BLOOD
ON THE
EQUATOR

BLOOD
ON THE
EQUATOR

A MURDER MYSTERY ACROSS THE BEAUTIFUL
LANDSCAPES OF ECUADOR

R.D.D. SMITH

Modelbenders Press

Blood on the Equator: A Murder Mystery Across the Beautiful Landscapes of Ecuador

AI Disclaimer: All the text, characters, and plot were created by a human author. Therefore, it is all covered by copyright. AI contributions are described in the "AI Disclosure" section at the end.

Modelbenders Press books may be purchased for business and promotional use. For information, please contact the publisher. Inquire with the author at **http://www.rddsmith.com/**

PRINTED IN THE UNITED STATES OF AMERICA

Interior and Cover Designed by Adina Cucicov at Flamingo Designs

The Library of Congress has cataloged the paperback edition:

Smith, R.D.D.
Blood on the Equator: A Murder Mystery Across the Beautiful
Landscapes of Ecuador
/ R.D.D. Smith–1st ed.
1. Murder Mystery, 2. Travelogue, 3. Thriller
I. R.D.D. Smith   II. Title.

Paperback ISBN 978-1-938590-35-1
Hardback ISBN 978-1-938590-36-8
eBook ISBN 978-1-938590-34-4

FICTION BY R.D.D. SMITH

Dr. Monica Gray, Medical Thriller Series
The Surgeon in the Mirror
Against a Viral Threat
Savior of the War Torn

Short Stories
The Surgeon's Genie
Freyja $AI

Global Runners Travelogue Series
Blood on the Equator

NONFICTION BY ROGER D. SMITH

Chief Technology Officer
Thinking About Innovation
In the Footsteps of Franklin
Advice Written on the Back of a Business Card
Patterns of Strength

TABLE OF CONTENTS

PREFACE: THE HISTORY OF ECUADOR

Ecuador is a country of striking contrasts and immense natural diversity, nestled on the northwest coast of South America. Its history stretches back thousands of years, with a rich tapestry woven from the threads of ancient indigenous cultures, Incan conquest, Spanish colonialism, and the country's eventual independence.

The history of pre-Inca Ecuador is lost in a misty tangle of time and legend, and the earliest historical details date back only as far as the 11th century AD. It is commonly believed that Asian nomads reached the South American continent by about 12,000 BC and were later joined by Polynesian colonizers. Centuries of tribal expansion, warfare, and alliances resulted in the relatively stable Duchicela lineage, which ruled more or less peacefully for nearly 150 years until the arrival of the Incas around 1450 AD.

Despite fierce opposition, the conquering Incas soon held the region, helped by strong leadership and policies of intermarriage. War over the inheritance of the new Incan kingdom weakened and divided the region on the eve of the arrival of the Spanish invaders.

The first Spaniards landed in northern Ecuador in 1526. Pizarro reached the country in 1532 and spread terror among the natives with the aid of his conquistadors' horses, armor, and weaponry. The Incan leader, Atahualpa, was ambushed, held for ransom, "tried" for his supposed crimes, and executed, effectively ending the Incan empire. The city of Quito held out for two years but was eventually razed by Atahualpa's general, Rumiñahui, who preferred destroying the city rather than losing it intact to the invading Spaniards. Quito was re-founded in December of 1534. Today, only one Inca site remains intact in Ecuador: Ingapirca, which is located to the north of Cuenca.

Spain ruled the colony from Lima, Peru, until 1739, when it was transferred to the viceroyalty of Colombia. After several attempts to liberate Ecuador from Spanish rule, Simón Bolívar finally achieved independence in 1822. Full constitutional sovereignty was gained in 1830. The country's internal history has since been marked by fierce rivalry and occasional open warfare between the church-backed conservatives in Quito and the liberals and socialists of Guayaquil.

In 1941, neighboring Peru invaded Ecuador and seized much of the country's Amazonian area. The "new" border between the two countries—although formally agreed upon and ratified by the 1942 Rio de Janeiro treaty—remains a matter of dispute. Border region skirmishes have occasionally flared up, usually around January, the month when the treaty was signed. The squabbling has died down in recent years, as both countries work to impress potential foreign investors, and a treaty is in the works that should finally bring an end to this dispute.

Despite its history of internal rivalry and border conflicts, life in Ecuador has remained peaceful in recent years. Ecuador is currently one of the safest countries to visit in South America.

Ecologically, Ecuador is one of the most diverse countries in the world, despite its relatively small size. It is famously split into four major regions: the Amazon rainforest, the Andean highlands, the coastal plains, and the Galápagos Islands, each with its unique ecosystems and species. The Amazon basin, known for its lush rainforest, hosts an incredible variety of flora and fauna, including numerous endemic species. The Andean region is characterized by high-altitude páramos and cloud forests, while the coastal areas feature beautiful beaches and mangroves. The Galápagos Islands, 900 kilometers west of the mainland, are renowned for their unique wildlife and were instrumental in the development of Charles Darwin's theory of evolution by natural selection.

However, the lush landscapes and rich ecosystems of Ecuador have been under threat because of extensive oil exploration and extraction. The oil industry expanded significantly in the 1970s after the discovery of large oil reserves in the Amazon basin. This development transformed the country's economy, with oil revenues fueling economic growth and development. Yet, this boon has not come without cost. The environmental impacts have been severe, particularly in the Amazon region, where oil extraction has led to deforestation, pollution, and disruption of indigenous communities.

Ecuador is a country where the past and present collide, where the natural world attracts tourists of all kinds, including groups who are eager to escape into its diverse landscapes.

CHAPTER 1

TUXEDO IN THE SHOWER

The squad room was a flurry of quiet activity, each detective engrossed in the glow of their individual computer screens. The ambient thrum of shoes on wooden floors and fingers on computer keyboards filled the air, a stark contrast to the tension that was about to break out.

"Moreno!" The voice was sharp, slicing through the monotony like a knife. No response.

"Moreno!!" This time, the voice was louder, more insistent.

The detectives at their desks pretended to be absorbed in their work, their eyes darting away from the source of the commotion. The sterile, white glow of the fluorescent lights cast harsh shadows on their faces, making the room feel colder, more clinical. Nobody wanted to attract the attention of Captain Adriane Castillo when he was in this kind of mood.

"Has anyone seen Detective Moreno? I need her in here right now!"

Silence hung in the air, thick and heavy. Before anyone could muster the courage to respond, a figure breezed into the room with the ease of a summer wind. Detective Jenn Moreno, with her characteristic beaming smile, appeared at Captain Castillo's side as if summoned by the sheer force of his frustration. At five foot five inches, she barely reached her captain's shoulder, but she was athletic and quick.

"Hi, boss. What can I do for you?" Her voice was light, almost musical, and her smile was unwavering. Though she had been a detective for five years, impressive for a woman of thirty-five, her spirit and enthusiasm were those of someone younger.

Captain Castillo, a tall man with a presence that filled the room, looked down at her, his initial irritation melting into a resigned amusement. He rolled his eyes heavenward. "Why am I always shouting to find you?

Can't you be at your desk like everyone else?" He swept his arm toward the other detectives, their postures slack as they sat under the oppressive lighting.

Jenn's smile flickered with a spark of mischief. "No crimes at my desk, boss. No clues in the drawers. I've got to be out there, with the people." She gave him a serious look, but her eyes twinkled with irreverence.

"Well, I need you to be out there right now. We got a call from the Hotel Quito. Someone found a body in one of the rooms. Take Carlos, get over there, and do some of that detective work we pay you for. Uniforms are already on site; they'll show you the room."

"Sure thing, sir. Any idea who the victim is?" Jenn removed her trusty notebook to capture the details.

"The report says he's wearing a tuxedo… in the shower."

"Kinky." Jenn mimed choking, her hands clasped around her throat, her tongue lolling out and eyes bulging in mock horror.

"Stop that! Just go!" Castillo's voice was half-exasperated, half-amused.

Jenn turned on her heel, her dark hair swinging as she called over her shoulder to her partner, "Grab your camera, Carlos. This one could be juicy."

"Sí, sí!" Carlos responded. The bushy-haired, bespectacled photographer for the station fell in line behind her.

As the pair vanished through the doorway, the tension in the squad room dissipated like fog in the sunlight. There was an audible exhale, a collective relief as life resumed its normal pace. Captain Castillo shook his head, a slight smile betraying his fondness for his most unconventional detective, before he retreated to the solitude of his office.

CHAPTER 2

PICTURING A MURDER

Jenn's Toyota Dart looked like a small white bug behind the giant tour bus that was parked in front of the Hotel Quito, one of the more ornate and stately hotels in the central city. It had once been the preferred destination for state dinners, but the more modern, glass-fronted, high-rise hotels had eclipsed it. However, groups who sought a more traditional Ecuadorian vibe for their meetings and travels still frequented it.

Pointing at the bus, Jenn asked, "Carlos, what's this thing doing here? This is a crime scene. We need to keep the area clear." Jenn's voice carried a mix of irritation and disbelief as she squinted at the chaotic scene, her brow furrowed in frustration at the apparent laxity of the uniformed officers.

Shoving the Quito Policia sign onto her dash, she swung out of the car and nearly collided with a tall gringo clad in an eye-catching ensemble of flamboyant, red running gear. His surprise was evident as he muttered a quick, "Excuso, por favor."

A procession followed him: individuals donned in yellow, green, blue, and red hues. Like a vividly colored parade, they streamed toward the bus, their laughter and chatter painting them unmistakably as American tourists. They seemed oblivious to the gravity of the situation, barely noticing Jenn and Carlos watching them from the curb. Jenn noted that they ranged in age from early twenties to well over sixty. But they were all dressed as if they were competing in a track and field championship event.

As the tide of tourists ebbed, Jenn approached the hotel's stone-faced security guard. "Who's that group?" she asked with her thumb pointed toward the bus.

"Running group from America," he replied, his gaze flicking to the badge at her belt.

"All of them? Even the older ones?" Jenn's tone was incredulous.

The guard merely shrugged and stepped aside, allowing Jenn and Carlos to pass without the usual security check for weapons, because, of course, they had weapons.

The uniformed officer in the lobby gave them directions to the murder scene, and the pair took the elevator up.

In the elevator, Jenn couldn't help but comment, "I could run faster than most of those gringos." She had actually been a competitive runner in secondary school and her first year of college, but she'd become much more casual as her major in criminal science became more demanding.

Carlos smiled, his eyes crinkling at the corners. "I like dinner better." He patted his stomach gently, a lighthearted moment amid their somber duty.

Arriving at room 1101, the pair entered and made their way to the bathroom, where the body was located. The victim appeared to be in his sixties, and was still dressed in an expensive-looking tuxedo, as promised. He was soaking wet, and small pools of water had accumulated around the body.

"No blood in the water, so he wasn't shot or stabbed." Jenn looked at the nearest officer. "Any weapons in the room?"

"No, ma'am. Just traveling clothes and suitcases as far as we can see. We didn't disturb anything."

"Maids?"

"One of them found the body. She claims she didn't touch anything, just screamed and ran to her boss."

Jenn nodded. Probably accurate. Most people didn't poke around when they found a body. Too shocking to the system. Or they were afraid that the person's ghost was still lurking about.

The maid, like many Ecuadorians, probably believed that the soul of the deceased lingered around the living for a period. So, it would make sense that she would be eager to get out of the immediate vicinity of the body. The soul was traditionally thought to be in a transitional state, navigating its way from the earthly plane to the afterlife. With a murder far from home, it would be difficult for the deceased's family and friends to aid in the peaceful transition of the soul. Traditional rituals were performed to prevent it from returning as a troubled spirit.

Carlos was taking pictures of everything in the room. He started with the body, capturing it from several angles. Then, he moved onto the shower fixtures, walls, and floor. He was very talented with the camera. Though they were just pictures of evidence, he made the most mundane scene look beautiful. Finished with the bathroom, he moved through the rest of the extensive suite.

Finally, Jenn asked the uniform, "Who is he?"

"Registration says Emilio Ortega."

Jenn's head snapped up from her notebook. "The Aspire Oil Ortega?"

This time, the uniform just shrugged.

Jenn's voice took on a lecturing tone at his dismissive gesture. "Emilio Ortega, CEO of Aspire Oil. He's been in the news shaking hands with the Minister of the Interior. He just signed a deal to exploit oil in the Amazon. Doesn't it ring a bell for you?"

The uniform shook his head and replied, "He's not a footballer. That's all I watch."

"Of course. Well, this case is going to be a big deal. Don't screw it up, or one of us will get fired." That got the officer's attention. It was hard to get into the policia service, and it was a great lifetime gig if you didn't screw it up.

"No, ma'am, I won't. *We* won't."

Jenn just nodded, as only time would tell if the officer was competent enough, and turned her attention back to her partner. "Carlos, are you almost finished? I want to look through some of this stuff."

"Jenn, come over here." The photographer was looking at something on the floor next to the bed. "What is that?"

Stooping closer, she said, "A button, maybe? Did you get a picture of it?"

"Of course, and from three different angles. It's best from over here with the light from the window glancing off it."

"It's just a button, Picasso." Wearing gloves, Jenn picked it up by its edge and examined it. Made of simple plastic, it had a tiny Ecuadorian flag on the face and a snap on the back. "Is this a lapel pin? Maybe to celebrate their oil deal with our country?"

"Could be." Carlos snapped another picture of it in her hand before she dropped it into an evidence bag.

The pair finished their examination of the room and stepped into the hall. She needed to let Castillo know what they were dealing with. She used her cell to call him directly.

"Chief, this is Moreno. We got the ID on the victim. Hold on to your lunch. It's Emilio Ortega, the CEO of Aspire Oil."

There was a series of loud expletives from the other end of the call, then a rapid fire set of instructions.

Jenn replied, "Yes. Yes. I will."

More instructions followed.

"Won't move until you get here. And we'll expect the Federales to show up," she said, referring to the Policía Nacional del Ecuador.

More cursing.

"I know, sir. Not what any of us wanted today… especially not Ortega."

Mumbling sounded from the phone.

"No, sir, not funny."

Jenn disconnected and looked around for her partner of the day. Carlos was crouching under a hallway lamp, capturing the pattern of light it cast on the wall. "Carlos! Not evidence."

"I know, but can you see how the light makes a pattern like a swan on the wall? It's exquisite."

He was right, though it was a detail that Jenn would never have noticed. Who looked at the world like that?

Pointing to the elevators, she said, "Lobby. We're talking to the manager." Carlos fell into step behind her, but his eyes continued to scan the hallway for interesting images he could capture.

In the manager's office, Jenn presented her credentials and began the typical line of questions: when did Ortega arrive, who was with him, did anyone ask about him, when was he last seen, who had access to the floor he was on? As was always the case, the manager's answers were generally useless.

Then, she asked, "And what group functions did you have in the hotel last night?"

"Oh, just two. Aspire Oil had the main banquet room. They needed to seat two hundred people. Very formal attire. The ladies came in the most beautiful dresses. The gentlemen were in tuxedos."

"And the purpose of the meeting?"

"They were celebrating the new oil deal in the Amazon. You know, the one that's been in the news." Jenn nodded as the manager continued talking. "Our pastry chef made the most amazing cake. It was an enormous green tree with monkeys, parrots, and snakes mixed through it. He even put a tarantula on the trunk. It was one of his best works. He was very proud."

Jenn interrupted by asking, "And Ortega was at the meeting all night?"

"He was the key speaker of the evening. Then, he was mixing with the crowd after the meal. The photographer has the sweetest picture of him eating a piece of the cake from the monkey's head. Our executive concierge said he went to his room early in the evening."

"Alone?"

"Sí, Señor Ortega's family did not come with him on this trip."

Jenn wondered if this was true. Hotel staff were expected to protect the privacy of their guests. Looking back at her notes, Jenn asked, "And what was the second group event?"

"That was a small group, maybe fifty people in the Highlands room. Very friendly. Everyone was happy."

Then, showing his distaste, he frowned slightly. "But very casual. Wearing shorts, sports shirts, and sandals. You know, we are accustomed to a more formal clientele at the Quito."

"What's the name of the group?" Jenn prompted. She was not interested in their clothing choices.

"Oh, yes. They are called Global Runners Travel, from America. All of them have rooms here in the hotel. Very lucrative for us."

"Did any of them have rooms on the same floor as Ortega?"

"Hmmm. I don't know for sure, but the front desk can tell you."

Pulling out the baggie containing the little pin, she showed it to the manager. "Have you seen anything like this before? Perhaps Aspire Oil execs wore them on their lapels?"

Looking at the plastic item, the manager's upper lip curled in disgust. "Certainly not! No one would put that plastic trinket on an expensive tuxedo. How horrible!" He looked away, as if the sight of it made him feel ill.

Jenn pocketed the offending item, stood, and handed him her card. "Thank you. Please, have your front desk send a list of the clients and their room numbers to this email address." Looking around, she caught Carlos staring intently out the window. He was looking at a little, white dog in a pink collar sniffing at the sidewalk. At least he had the good sense not to snap pictures during the interview.

"Carlos, banquet room, now."

CHAPTER 3

DAMNED FEDERALES

In the dimly lit, sparsely decorated office of Captain Castillo, the ambiance was only marginally more welcoming than the sterile squad room outside. The walls, a subdued shade of gray, were punctuated by several framed commendations and a solitary photograph of Castillo shaking hands with the former mayor of Quito. A pair of glass-fronted cabinets, crafted from dark, somber wood and filled with untouched books, stood as silent witnesses of the people who had passed through this office. Detective Jenn Moreno suspected these relics hadn't felt human hands in decades, their contents as forgotten as old secrets.

"Moreno, the federales are all over this case. They don't trust you, me, or anyone in the Quito Policia force to handle it," Castillo said, his voice echoing slightly in the cool, sparse room.

Strictly speaking, the Quito Policia and the federales were all part of the same national police force. But where Castillo's unit focused on crime in the central part of Quito city, the department that handled crimes spanning the entire country were often referred to as "the federales." That department encouraged the separate distinction, as it added to their own mystique and perceived power. They rarely intervened in local criminal investigations, even murders, preferring to focus on larger issues with organized crime, drug trafficking, kidnapping, and anything connected to the national government.

"Of course, Chief. A corporate executive tied to our highest government officials, very sensitive stuff," Jenn replied, her mind racing ahead to the implications.

"This information is confidential, but they're convinced it was an internal power struggle. Someone at Aspire Oil is angling for the top position. They've shortlisted a few executives," Castillo disclosed, his eyes scanning a document on his desk as if to memorize its contents.

Jenn nodded, her thoughts weaving through possibilities. "Sí, that's one angle. But what if it's a maneuver by the Ecuadorian government? A ploy to renegotiate the oil deals, maybe shift the exploration sites, or even control which vendors profit?"

Castillo's gaze sharpened, and his voice dropped to a whisper when he said, "Don't even hint at that. That's exactly why they don't trust us. An overzealous detective starts probing about government ties." He gestured in a circle with his finger, then pointed at Jenn. "Next thing you know, it's all over the press. The public gets restless, demands changes, and chaos ensues."

"So, we just ignore that possibility?" Jenn challenged.

"We have to. That's the federales' call," Castillo stated firmly.

"Fine. Can I at least follow up on local leads?"

"You mean the maids, the hotel chef, some random street lunatic? Yes, those are all yours, but steer clear of corporate and government threads. And keep out of the federalcs' way," he instructed.

Jenn glanced toward the squad room, noticing two nondescript figures who were clearly with the federales, not the local department. They had commandeered a desk as if they now worked here. "Those two?"

"Yes, those two. They're here because we're near the hotel and we have a secure connection to the federal network. They'll be out of our hair soon… hopefully," Castillo murmured, almost to himself.

Jenn scrutinized the federal agents again, more closely this time. They were unremarkable in every way, clad in sharply tailored, yet utterly forgettable attire, the very image of bureaucratic anonymity. "I already don't like them. They look as dull as they probably sound."

Castillo, puzzled by her comment, simply shook his head. "You can play around with this case for a week. We need to show diligence—no angles overlooked; no stone unturned. So, go turn over some stones… but small stones. But don't touch the big ones, or you might get crushed."

"And Carlos? Can he help?" Jenn asked, already moving toward the door.

"Sure, whatever. Now, get out of here. I've got a meeting with the feds soon, and I'd rather they didn't run into you," Castillo concluded, dismissing her with a wave.

Jenn exited without hesitation, catching the furtive glances of the federal agents while doing so. She returned no pleasantries, eager to escape any bureaucratic taint they might carry.

About an hour later, in the bustling lobby bar of the Hotel Quito, Jenn and Carlos claimed a secluded table, their makeshift command center. Here, amid the low hum of conversations and clinking glasses, they planned their investigation.

They began with the hotel's eleventh-floor cleaning staff, including Jasmine, who had discovered the body. They extracted every scrap of information that she and her colleagues could remember. Finally, they concluded the interview by instructing the cleaning staff to report anything out of the ordinary. "When you're working, if you find anything unusual, we want to know about it. This is a serious criminal investigation. You won't get in trouble for cooperating with us."

"Señorita, we always see things that are unusual. People in hotels are very strange." Jasmine didn't elaborate, but Jenn's imagination could fill in the blanks.

"No, none of those things. Only if it seems it could be used to kill someone."

Jasmine nodded. "Ah, yes. Like guns, knives, drugs. But not ropes."

"No, not ropes," Jenn confirmed.

"That's good. There are so many ropes." Jasmine shook her head in disbelief at the things the housekeepers saw and had to clean up. Not for the first time, Jenn was silently thankful that she had chosen law enforcement.

Regrouping at their lobby table later that day, Jenn and Carlos reviewed their progress. "We've talked to the cleaning staff, the chef's team, security, and front desk. Who's left?"

Carlos counted off on his fingers. "Maintenance, management, and the concierge. Maybe the gift shop and groundskeepers?"

Before Jenn could answer, there was a roar of conversation coming in through the front doors. It was the rainbow river of Americans pouring out of the bus on the curb. They looked much filthier than when they left. Their shoes and legs were dirty. Some of them were still wet with sweat. As the air from the open door reached their table, Jenn caught an earthy scent.

Carlos asked, "What about them?" Instinctively, he pointed his camera toward the group and began snapping pictures.

"Hmm, maybe. Sure, why not? We have time." Looking at the room list, she highlighted the ones on the "murder floor," as she had started calling it. "Three of them are on the same floor. Let's wait for them to get cleaned up, then we'll knock on their doors. That will liven up their vacation, I'm sure."

"Who are we talking to?" Carlos asked, nodding at the paper in Jenn's hand.

"We'll start with the rooms closest to Gomez's suite and work our way down the hall. First stop, 1104, Joe and Christie Adams from Minnesota. Then, 1107, Karen vonScheck… something. Too many letters to pronounce. Finally, 1115, Allen Shur from Argentina." Jenn pointed to the last name. "Surprising. I thought this group was all Americans?"

Carlos stood. "Shall we go up?"

"Not you. You stay here and watch the lobby. I'm taking one of the uniforms from the car out front. Much bigger impact when they see a uniform at the door. More likely to slip up or wet themselves." She smiled in anticipation of how much fun it was going to be.

CHAPTER 4

SURPRISE VISITOR

Knock. Knock. Knock.

"Um, who is it?"

"Policia. Please, open the door." The uniformed officer's voice was deep and authoritative, exactly what Jenn had hoped for in setting the tone of this encounter.

"What? You're kidding."

"No, Señor Adams. This is the Quito Policia."

From within the confines of the small hotel room, whispers seeped out as Jenn observed her uniformed colleague. His attempt at a reassuring smile did little to soften the severity etched into his weather-worn face, another advantage of bringing him along on this visit.

The door cracked open slightly, revealing a wary eye. "Honey, it really is the police," Joe Adams called back into the room before swinging the door wide open, revealing his full, slightly disheveled appearance. He stared at the large, stern-looking police officer.

Jenn spoke next. "Excuse us for disturbing you, Mr. Adams. We have a few questions." It was then that Joe tore his gaze from the uniformed cop, noticing her presence for the first time.

"Of course. How do we do this?" Clearly, he was unaccustomed to encounters with law enforcement.

"Can we come in?" Jenn inquired smoothly.

"The room is pretty small for all of us," Joe replied, his voice tinged with discomfort at the thought of the police intruding into his private space.

"You can come to my office at the police station, if that would be better," Jenn offered and watched him weigh his options.

"No. No. We can talk here. Please, come in." Joe stepped aside, opening the door wider.

Jenn entered, followed by her uniformed colleague, her lips curving into a satisfied smile at the American's compliance.

"This is my wife, Christie." Joe gestured toward a woman, who looked equally perturbed at the presence of Jenn and the street cop. "Um, what can we do for you? Is there a problem?" His eyes flickered between Jenn and her imposing partner, unsure who commanded more authority.

Jenn assessed the pair. Early thirties, physically fit runners, expensive running clothes by Ecuadorian standards. Both were nervous. She decided to alleviate some tension. "Not a problem for you." The couple visibly relaxed, their shoulders dropping as they let out silent sighs of relief.

As her eyes swept the room, Jenn took in the typical setup of a traveler's accommodation: a queen-sized bed dominated the space, surrounded by modest furniture cluttered with scattered garments, while suitcases attempted to blend inconspicuously with the shadows. Her glance was casual but perceptive, searching for any anomaly.

Her focus then returned to the couple, especially Christie. "Were you aware that a crime occurred on this floor last night?"

"No. We hadn't heard that, but we saw police officers in the lobby this morning when we left. Is it something serious?" Christie's voice was tinged with concern.

"You didn't see the news today? It's been quite well-covered by all the local stations."

Christie shook her head. "No. We're on vacation, and we don't speak Spanish. Oh, and we went for a run in the metropolitan park this morning, so we were busy."

"Ah, Parque Metropolitano. And you enjoyed it?" Jenn was softening them up for harder questions.

"Very much. It was heavily forested and a rougher terrain than we expected for something right here in town." Christie looked at Joe for confirmation. He nodded in agreement.

"Yes, even the city has a lot of natural beauty to offer." Then Jenn switched to the business at hand. "We're here because there was a murder in room 1101 sometime last night." Jenn paused to let the gravity of the information settle.

"Oh, my God! We didn't know." Alarm flickered between them, their eyes darting to the officer, perhaps expecting a sudden movement and the appearance of handcuffs.

"I have a few questions," Jenn continued, without waiting for their invitation to proceed. "Did you hear anything unusual in the hall or through the walls last night? You know, like an argument, loud banging, doors slamming, that kind of thing."

Both shook their heads, seeking reassurance from each other, then jointly responded, "No. I don't think so."

"What time were you in this room last night?"

Joe took the lead this time. "We were at a reception downstairs until late. It was, like, eleven o'clock when we came up here."

"What kind of reception?" Though she already knew what the event was about thanks to the hotel's manager, she wanted to see if the Americans would be truthful.

"We're with Global Runners Travel. They had a welcome reception to start our vacation trip last night. Everyone was there. You can ask. Lots of people saw us at the dinner." Joe's nervousness caused him to construct an alibi to defend their innocence.

Jenn, experienced with this reaction, noted it but remained neutral. "I'm sure you were. We'll check on that later. And you're sure you didn't see or hear anything that could help us with the investigation? It was a murder. The killer might have bumped into you in the hall? Maybe knocked on your door by mistake?" Her questions, seemingly innocuous, were designed to unsettle, to probe deeper into their emotions.

"Oh, my God! Are we in danger? Do we need to change hotels?" Christie's anxiety was palpable, her voice quivering.

"No, no, honey. It's okay. We're moving tomorrow, anyway," Joe reassured her, and in doing so, inadvertently revealed more of their plans.

"Moving? Where are you going? You're not running off on me, are you?" Jenn's tone was light, but pointed.

"No, we're not running away. It's the planned itinerary. We start in Quito, then move around to run in different parts of the country," Joe explained hastily, his words rushing out as he attempted to clarify their travel plans.

"I see. And where will you be tomorrow?" Jenn raised her eyebrows.

"Ibarra, I think."

"What hotel?"

"I don't know. Global Runners handles all that. We just get on the bus, and they take us to the next stop."

Jenn looked around the room again. "So, you need to pack up tonight?"

"Yes, but that only takes us a few minutes," Joe answered.

Jenn's eyes landed on something she'd missed on her first scan. She walked over to the desk and picked up a small plastic button. It had the letters "GR" on the front and a snap on the back.

Holding it up, she turned to Christie and asked, "What is this?"

"It's a bib board."

Jenn raised her eyebrows, indicating that she didn't know what that meant.

"Oh, sorry. Runners use those to attach their race numbers to their shirts." Christie looked around the room and picked up a brightly colored T-shirt. "Like this." The shirt had a paper number attached to it with several of the buttons. Christie unsnapped one and then re-snapped it together to show the button's purpose.

"That's really interesting. I haven't seen that before. I'm not sure we have those in Ecuador."

"They're kind of new in America, but you can buy them if you don't like to use safety pins."

"And these are custom made for your group?" Jenn asked.

"Yeah. Global Runners gave them to everyone on the trip," Christie answered.

"That's nice. Are there other designs?"

"A full set is four, each with a different picture on it."

"Can I keep this?" Jenn looked at Christie with a serious expression.

"Um, I guess so," the American woman replied.

"Thank you for your cooperation. If we need anything else, we'll find you in Ibarra." With that, Jenn nodded toward the door and she and the street cop left the room, closing the door behind them. They stopped in the hall and remained inches from the door.

They could hear Joe's voice when he exclaimed, "Great! You just gave away my bib board. Now, how am I going to attach my bib?"

"Like I was going to say no to the police? You saw the look on her face. She's small, but I swear, she was scarier than the big, uniformed guy."

Joe changed the subject. "There was a murder right across the hall from us. Was it random? They could have chosen our room. Pretended to be room service, then charged in and done…whatever."

"Stop it, Joe. That's not funny. I'm searching for more details now."

Moments of silence ensued before the couple spoke again.

"Wow! Here it is," Christie said. "Emilio Ortega, the CEO of Aspire Oil. Murdered in his hotel room. Doing deals with the government in Ecuador. Police don't have a suspect."

"Aspire Oil? My company does work for them. We make some equipment for their oil rigs," Joel said.

"Really? Could she suspect that you're connected to Ortega because of that?"

"No way! He's the CEO. I'm just an engineer for some remote supplier."

In the hall, Jen was jotting all this information down. *This is the best job in the world,* she thought to herself. Then she turned to the uniform and said, "Next room."

Knocking on room 1107, the pair repeated their act. This time, they met a veterinarian with pictures of dogs on her luggage and laptop.

Jenn varied the script a little by asking, "Do vets travel with surgical supplies?"

"Oh, yes, of course. I have basic examination tools, pet-specific bandages, some suturing needles, that kind of thing."

"Scalpels?"

"No! That wouldn't get through security."

Jenn nodded. "I guess it wouldn't. Medicines?"

"A few. Basic antibiotics. You know, in case I see an animal that I can help on the trip."

"Antibiotics that require a syringe to administer?"

The enthusiasm dropped out of Karen Von-something's voice. "Well, yes. Most of them are."

"Show me." The request was firm.

Karen opened a small bag that contained two syringes and four small bottles of clear fluid. She was obviously very nervous now. Jenn could see little beads of sweat on her upper lip.

"And airport security allows these?" Jenn looked skeptical.

"They do. The medicine and equipment are the same that a diabetic might carry for their personal treatment. Sometimes, they ask to see my medical credentials. That usually clears it up if they have any questions."

"The same goes for international travel?"

"Diabetes treatment is the same in most countries." Karen sounded defensive, as though she wasn't used to being questioned about her decisions, and Jenn made a mental note of her behavior.

"That's fine. I don't know anything about the laws for that in Ecuador. I'm just interested in the murder down the hall."

There were a few more questions before the officers took their leave. Just like before, they waited outside the door for a few minutes.

This time, all they heard was, "Oh, shit." Then, it was quiet in room 1107.

CHAPTER 5

BREAKING DOWN DOORS

In the shadowed confines of their makeshift headquarters in the lobby bar, Detective Jenn Moreno and her partner Carlos sat with steaming cups of coffee, plotting their next move. The American runners had piqued Jenn's interest, not just from their proximity to the crime scene, but from their oddly timed excursions around the country.

"Three Americans, Carlos. Three on the same floor during the night of the murder. Coincidence?" Jenn murmured while her eyes scanned the case notes strewn across the table.

Carlos, ever the skeptic, shrugged. "Could be tourists being tourists. But I'll check their alibis for the night, just to be safe."

Amid the clatter of arriving and departing guests, Jenn approached the concierge desk to gather more nuanced insights about their suspects. The concierge, a well-dressed man with an impeccable posture, greeted her with a cautious smile.

"Detective Moreno, how can I assist you today?" he inquired, his voice a blend of curiosity and wariness.

"I need information on the American running group. Anything unusual about their stay? Their activities or requests?" Jenn asked in a deliberately casual tone.

The concierge paused, his eyes flickering to a log book before responding, "They were quite enthusiastic about their runs, always asking for local trails and shopping. Nothing out of the ordinary, though they did ask a lot about the safety of the areas they visited."

"Did they meet with anyone else here? Any local contacts?" Jenn pressed.

"Just the usual tour guides. But there was one local runner who joined them yesterday. I think he works for the local company who's guiding their entire trip," the concierge added. In doing so, he offered a new thread for Jenn to pull.

"Name and contact details, if you have them," Jenn requested, handing him her notebook.

The concierge dutifully scribbled down the information, his hand steady but quick. "Here you are. Anything else, Detective?"

"That'll be all for now, thank you." Jenn pocketed the notebook, her mind already racing with the new lead.

After Jenn went back over to inform Carlos of what she had learned, their discussion was abruptly cut short by a phone call from Captain Castillo. His voice was tense, laced with urgency.

"Moreno, fresh development. The federales just pulled high-grade explosives from a locker at the airport. Registered under a fake ID, but the connections to Aspire Oil are too obvious to ignore. They're serving a search warrant to one of the execs today."

Jenn's pulse quickened, but she needed to tell her boss about the Americans. "Chief, I have something on the American runners."

"No time for that. We're supporting this mission. Get back here now. We're leaving in an hour," Castillo commanded before hanging up.

Turning to Carlos, Jenn's face was full of excitement at the prospect of action. "Change of plans. I'm going on a raid. I mean, a premises search. Whatever's happening, it's bigger than we thought."

The duo hurriedly left the hotel, their steps quick and purposeful. As they navigated the crowded streets of Quito, Jenn couldn't shake off a nagging thought—the American runners, the local guide, and now explosives. The pieces were there, but they didn't seem to fit together.

As they approached the imposing structure of the police station, the air was thick with tension. Jenn and Castillo, now clad in bulletproof vests boldly emblazoned with "Policia" on both the chest and back, prepared themselves for the operation. Jenn noted two federales who were also armored in full riot gear. Their weapons—a mix of shotguns and automatic rifles—gleamed ominously under the harsh fluorescent lights. Accompanied by four equally well-equipped agents, the group seemed ready for a siege rather than a simple legal procedure.

"Chief, why are they dressed to go to war and we just get vests?" Jenn questioned, her voice echoing slightly in the cavernous room.

"Obviously, we'll be tagging along from behind. They do the dirty work. We just watch and support," Castillo responded, his tone suggesting it was par for the course, though Jenn found the entire setup disproportionate for the task at hand.

The convoy of police and federal vehicles made its way to a secluded hacienda nestled in an affluent enclave of Quito. The sun cast long shadows on the ground as they parked discreetly a block away; the vehicles clustered around a massive Hummer that seemed out of place with its imposing bulk.

The federales' commander, a stern figure in tactical gear, gestured for silence and attention. "Listen up. We've sent three of our men around to the back of the compound. We have three more here at the front, plus all you local policia. We suspect the compound's security guards will not let us walk right in," he briefed, his voice low but still carrying throughout the group.

Jenn exchanged a worried glance with Castillo. The operation was shaping up to be more of an assault on a fortified location than the mere execution of a search warrant.

The commander laid out the plan with clinical precision. "Castillo, you and your young officer, you drive up to the gate. Exit the vehicle and inform the guards that you have a search warrant. If they let you in, then we'll just drive up behind you and go in. No problems."

Jenn's discomfort was palpable. They were not backup; they were the spearhead of the entire mission. "And what if they don't let us in? Then, what happens?" she asked, her voice tinged with anxiety.

Annoyance flickered across the federale commander's face. "Then we'll handle it from our positions. You just do your part and try not to get in our way," he retorted before commanding everyone to prepare to move out.

Castillo, attempting to reassure Jenn, led her back to their car. "We just serve the warrant. Then we let the feds do the rest."

"Yeah, that's all—except we're in the middle of the firing zone," Jenn muttered as they approached the formidable gates of the hacienda.

Upon arrival, they were greeted not by a welcoming committee, but by two imposing guards armed with AK-47 rifles. "Alto!" one guard commanded, stopping any further advance.

Castillo stepped forward, the search warrant in hand. "We have a search warrant for these premises," he announced. His voice was steady, despite the palpable tension.

The guard met Castillo's declaration with a stony stare. "No. You may not enter. Go back to your little cop house," he dismissed them, gesturing with the rifle for emphasis.

"Are you defying a judge's order and the policia?" Castillo challenged.

The guard's expression remained unchanged. "Sí," he replied simply, and blocked their path.

At that moment, the tension broke with the sound of two loud booms. Jenn watched in disbelief as the guards collapsed, struck by non-lethal beanbags—a testament to the federales' unexpected restraint. Two agents rushed from cover and zip tied both guards' hands before they could recover.

As the dust settled, a massive Hummer bulldozed through the gates, the commander behind the wheel, his face set in determination. "Get in," he instructed through the open window, though not to Jenn and Castillo. "Not you two. You follow in your car."

With the outer defenses breached, the convoy advanced toward the grandiose main house. The atmosphere was electric, charged with adrenaline and a sense of impending confrontation. At the door, the federales wasted no time. "Señor Delgado, this is the Ecuadorian Federal Service. We're here to search your house. Would you like to open the door? Or shall we blow it apart?" One agent was already applying explosives to the door jams, just in case.

The threat of explosives was enough. The door swung open, revealing a flustered man who protested vehemently, but to no avail. The commander, unfazed, presented the search warrant. "Our invitation to search your house."

"This is outrageous! The Minister of the Interior will hear about this. You'll be lucky if you just lose your job, Commander. Aspire Oil is bringing millions to this country, money the government needs to pay your salary."

As they entered, the commander laid out the stakes clearly. "Señor Delgado, we found explosives in a locker at the airport. These are exactly the kinds of explosives that your company uses in its oil operations. Therefore, we believe you and your company are involved in some unauthorized activities. Perhaps those explosives were meant for the home of the Minister of the Interior? Perhaps he will not be so quick to defend you when he hears of this news?"

"I know nothing about explosives. I'm an executive vice president at the company," Delgado protested, his voice a mix of indignation and fear. But his words did little to sway the determined federales as they began their meticulous search of the mansion.

Interrupting, the commander pressed further, "And you're next in line for the CEO position now that Emilio Ortega is deceased?"

"Potentially. However, that decision is in the hands of the board," the executive responded.

"Or perhaps," the commander speculated, "they conspired with you to eliminate Ortega, ensuring your promotion and doubling their financial returns from corporate deals?"

"That accusation is unfounded. You cannot operate a global oil company with such tactics."

"We'll see about that," the commander retorted.

Just then, one agent approached the main hall, holding up an artifact. "Commander, look at this." He presented a long tube adorned with tribal markings and vibrant feathers. In his other hand, he held several large, feathered darts.

"A blowgun from the Shuar tribe of the Amazon, and these darts—possibly coated with poison from tree frogs?" the commander proposed.

"These were a gift from the tribe, in recognition of the benefits we're bringing to their area. They wouldn't give us poisoned darts meant merely for display," the executive argued.

"You underestimate their traditions. They equip even their children with poison-tipped darts for hunting. Imagine if you, or someone else—perhaps Emilio Ortega—had accidentally been pricked by one."

A gasp filled the room. "I could have been poisoned? I never would have accepted them had I known," the executive exclaimed, his face turning pale with the shock of the potential danger.

"We'll send these for testing to confirm if they are, indeed, poisoned. If so, you'll have more explaining to do," the commander stated.

As the operation concluded, more agents congregated in the foyer, each carrying various items now deemed suspicious: a handgun, a bottle of pills, assorted documents, and an antique Spanish sword.

Outside, as they prepared to leave, the commander commended his team, "Excellent work, everyone. Even the local police did well today. We've seized multiple items that could be linked to criminal activities, including paperwork concerning their compound in the jungle."

Fuming, Castillo headed to their vehicle with Jenn Morales close behind him. "Those damn federales! They used us as decoys to provoke the guards. Once the guards reacted, it gave them justification to escalate. We were nearly caught in the middle of it."

Jenn, though equally upset, masked her concerns with a forced grin and patted her bulletproof vest. "At least we were bulletproof," she joked, trying to lighten the mood.

On their drive back, Jenn resumed a conversation they had started earlier. "Chief, about those Americans—I think there's more to their story. I want to keep an eye on them." She shared details from her interviews during the drive. By the time they arrived at the station, Castillo had consented to her continuing the investigation and tracking their movements. Jenn strategically omitted what she knew about their plans to leave Quito the next day. She knew he would not approve a jaunt around the country.

CHAPTER 6

UNDERCOVER RUNNER

"Gather round, Global Runners. We're going to cover the plan for the day," announced a petite British woman with an authoritative tone. Jenn knew her only as Zuri, a name she recalled vaguely among the myriad details she'd memorized for her assignment.

Zuri's voice carried over the assembled crowd, a mixture of excitement and routine etched into her instructions. "Today will be like most days. Pack your luggage, and remember that it goes under the bus. Carry your day bag with the essentials you'll need after the run and for our activity." A few heads bobbed in understanding, but many in the group were wrapped up in their own conversations, hardly paying attention to the briefing.

"These are our local partners," Zuri continued, gesturing toward a group of locals led by a man named Patricio. "Patricio's team plans our running routes, leads the runs, and moves ahead of us to ensure our hotels and meals are ready." She motioned for Patricio to take over, and he began introducing his team in a blend of Spanish and English.

Jenn was third in line. Her hair was pulled back into a no-nonsense ponytail, her face slightly obscured by glasses. She donned a GR hat and shirt marked "Staff." It was a flimsy disguise, she thought, but it would have to suffice until she could ensure those in the know kept her secret—that she was investigating a murder.

Her integration into the group had been seamless, a concoction of circumstance and clever manipulation. Using the information provided by the hotel concierge, Jenn and Carlos had paid a visit to one of the guides, explaining that he would call in sick and couldn't continue with the trip. Then, they gave him the script and instructed him to call Patricio to recommend his good friend Jenn Moreno as an ideal replacement. As simple as that, Jenn was now part of the traveling tour group. She knew this level of infiltration was beyond what Castillo had approved when he said she could follow them. But forgiveness could come later, especially if she uncovered a killer.

Patricio introduced her role without fanfare. "Jenn will be in charge of bus snacks, aid stations, and the food tables at the finish line." He then continued with the introductions.

Jenn casually observed the Adams couple to gauge any sign of recognition. Fortunately, they, like most of the group, were engrossed in their own discussions. This anonymity was a blessing, providing her with more time to blend in unnoticed.

Once everyone was aboard the bus, Jenn stowed her box of snacks and took a seat in the back row, strategically placing herself amidst a cluster of runners. It was an ideal spot for eavesdropping and starting casual conversation.

"I'm pleased you all came to my country. You will see some beautiful landscapes during the trip," Jenn said to a pair of women.

"I'm Toni, and this is my sister, Lisa. We love these trips. This is our third," the woman replied. Then, showing her own curiosity, she asked, "Are you from Quito?"

"My family originally comes from the highlands, where we will run today. I live in Quito now—more jobs and better nightlife here. We're actually running close to my family's farm. We grow plantains and potatoes. What do you do?" Jenn inquired, weaving bits of truth into her cover story to make it sound more convincing.

"We're both corporate lawyers for the oil industry," Lisa responded.

Jenn's interest piqued. "Any companies here in Ecuador?"

"Probably. Most are global, so they might have operations here," Lisa explained nonchalantly.

"Have you heard of Aspire Oil? They're making big moves here," Jenn asked casually.

"Yes, of course. They're well known. Aspire is often the first to break into a new country when there's the scent of oil in the air," said Lisa.

Then, Toni added, "Did you know they had a large banquet at our hotel on the first day? Their CEO was even there to speak."

Jenn feigned ignorance. "No, I wasn't at the hotel that day." She quickly shifted back to their previous travel experiences. "Your third trip? Where else have you been?"

"Iceland and Costa Rica. Both were incredible," Toni recalled, and her eyes lit up with the memories.

"Do many people come back on multiple trips?" Jenn probed in an attempt to understand the group dynamics better.

"Yes, they do. In fact, we know several people here from those previous trips," Toni said and pointed out others on the bus.

"Is anyone here on their first GR trip?" Jenn thought this information could be very helpful. Joining this specific trip for their first time would be one hell of a coincidence, after all.

"Those two at the front, Alice and Cathy, over there. Probably others as well." Toni pointed at the women she was referring to.

Jenn made a mental note of the names and faces. She would write this down later when she was alone. "Snacks?" she offered the sisters.

As they continued to converse, Jenn learned about the women's lives and their expectations for this journey. She shared her own fabricated experiences of studying in the city and working for the local water department, a cover close enough to her real life to be credible.

On her other side, she chatted with a couple from Montana, seasoned travelers but with no direct ties to the oil industry. Jenn mentally cataloged each conversation, alert to any detail that might connect these seemingly innocuous tourists to her investigation. She counted eight of the Americans that she had now met, and she was surprised at how many had traits that made them possible suspects.

The bus hummed along, leaving the bustling streets of Quito and climbing into the verdant landscapes as it headed toward its first significant stop: the equator.

SHADOWS AND SUNDIALS

Jenn's responsibilities as a makeshift tour guide were momentarily paused as the bus halted at Quitsato, a renowned tourist destination known for its sundial and solar museum. While the other tourists eagerly disembarked, Jenn lingered at the back of the group, using the brief moments of solitude to scribble down her observations in a small, worn notebook. Then she quickly tapped out a message to Captain Castillo and Carlos, updating them on her progress and location. She was still too close to Quito to reveal what she was doing to Castillo. He would certainly call her back if he knew.

Jenn was no stranger to Quitsato. Having grown up nearby, she had visited the sundial on several school trips and had brought visiting friends to the museum, located just a short drive from Quito. The site was modest compared to other equatorial attractions in Ecuador, yet it boasted a distinct focus on science that appealed to her analytical mind.

As the group congregated around a detailed model of the Earth and sun, the resident scientist began his presentation. He recounted the journey of French astronomers who, in 1736, had ventured to Ecuador's tall peaks to measure the Earth's circumference. His words painted a vivid scene of historical adventurers against the backdrop of Ecuador's high mountains, which were perfect for celestial observations, unlike the dense jungles cloaking the equator in other countries.

The explanation visibly impressed Toni, one of the lawyer sisters. "This is a much better explanation than anything I ever got in school." Pointing to the intricate Earth model in front of the group, she added, "Every school should have a model like that."

Jenn, like most Ecuadorians, was quite proud when her homeland impressed visitors from countries that were much richer than her own, especially those from America.

The tour proceeded onto the giant stone mosaic sundial, but Jenn drifted toward the edges of the group, drawn instead to the tranquility of the extensive agave garden. She savored the solitude, knowing the runners would be preoccupied with snapping photos by the sundial's towering orange pillar.

As she meandered among the agaves, her ears caught the distant calls for the group to align themselves along the equator for a photo. Lost in her thoughts about the investigation, she bent down to examine a particularly striking, red-tipped mountain agave. Suddenly, a deep "thump" shattered the calm. Spinning around, Jenn saw a large rock tumbling down from the nearby tower, crashing into the garden. She narrowly dodged it, leaping aside as the rock continued its destructive path, eventually smashing into a nearby wooden building.

"Holy shit!" Jenn exclaimed, her eyes darting up to the now-empty top of the tower where the rock had dislodged.

Quitsato staff and several tourists rushed over. A concerned staff member reached her first. "Señorita, are you all right?"

"Sí, sí. It missed me. But it was very scary. Very close," Jenn replied, and she could feel her heart still racing at what could have happened.

An older man, dressed in formal attire, approached with an apologetic tone. "We are very sorry. I don't know how such a large rock could have been loose and ready to fall. Thank heavens you were not hurt. We will close the area and send our people to check and secure every stone."

Jenn's gaze returned to the tower, skepticism creeping into her thoughts. Was what happened truly an accident, or something intentional?

Patricio, her current boss, joined her, concern etched across his features. "Are you okay? Do you need a medical exam?"

"No, no. I'm fine. It was just a close call."

"You're good to continue with the group?"

"Yes, of course."

"Good. Then, you can have the snack box ready as everyone boards the bus. You know Americans — always hungry."

Jenn nodded, her mind still replaying the incident as she headed to the bus. Inside the slightly damaged building, the scientist continued his lecture. "Do you know the origins of the word 'north?' It comes from the German word 'nord,' which means 'left.' Early astronomers oriented their eye to the sunrise and labeled the directions from that starting point. Hence, north is on your left, 'sud' or south on your right, and 'est' is the primary direction where the sun rises." This speech was the basis for his challenge on the conventional view of the solar system. Jenn had heard it all before, but the entrenched errors of history were too deep to correct now, despite the efforts of dedicated scientists in remote outposts like this one.

At the bus, Jenn donned sunglasses and a cap, readying a box of snacks as the runners re-boarded. "Snack?" she offered, scanning each face for any hint of recognition or emotion.

Most passed by without a second glance. However, Allen, the photographer, paused, placing a hand on her shoulder with a concerned smile. In Spanish, he urged her, "Chiquita, be careful. You must not get hurt with us. We would be very sad." She wondered whether his words were kind or an ominous warning.

CHAPTER 8

BREATHLESS HEIGHTS

As the sun shone warm in the late morning sky, a heavily laden bus heaved its way up the serpentine roads to Cotacachi Cayapas. Inside, the group of international runners exchanged anxious glances and stories about the daunting challenge ahead—a race at dizzying altitudes.

Karen, with her sea-level lungs, wrapped her arms around herself as though the very thought of the upcoming run could make her breathless. "9,000 feet and climbing! That's crazy. I live at one hundred feet elevation," she exclaimed, her voice tinged with a mix of excitement and trepidation.

Beside her, Alice shone like a beacon of enthusiasm. Her eyes twinkled with the thrill of adventure. "Denver's above 5,000, and I go up into the Rockies regularly. We have lots of peaks higher than this one," she chimed in confidently.

Karen turned to Alice with her eyebrows raised in a silent challenge. "And you run those?"

Alice's smile didn't waver, but her response was a touch more modest. "Well, no. But we do hike them."

Dave, brimming with competitive energy, couldn't contain himself. "I got this one. We run mountains in Phoenix. So, I just have to deal with the elevation change, and I'll be fine." He was clearly itching for a course that would test his mettle; the placid trails of Quito's metropolitan preserve had offered no such satisfaction.

Meanwhile, Jenn, a local with the lean, muscular build of someone born to run these highlands, had selected her favorite running shoes. They were her bond to the earth, her allies in the dance over terrain that was both friend and foe. She was determined to carve a few miles into these trails, even if her undercover role limited her freedom.

"Patricio, this is my home province. Can I run a few miles?" she asked, her voice carrying the subtle strength of someone who knew the land like the lines on their hands.

Patricio turned around with an expression of mild surprise. "You really want to run with them?" His eyes searched hers, trying to decipher her motives.

Jenn's smile was mischievous, a flicker of her inner cunning that made her excellent at her job. Patricio relented upon seeing it. "Okay, you can run. But first, you set up the finish line snack table." He gestured toward the empty tables, awaiting provisions. With his own conspiratorial grin, he said, "And don't beat the leaders. If you come in first, it's back to Quito for you."

Laughter was their shared language as Jenn hurried to prepare the tables. She grabbed a water bottle, its weight reassuring in her hand.

The air thrummed with anticipation as the first official race of the vacation trip loomed. A tall, sinewy American with the posture of someone accustomed to leading from the front jostled to the starting line alongside a man whose build resembled a fortress of muscle. Jenn had yet to make their acquaintance. She wove herself into the heart of the pack, where Christie and Karen, both previously interviewed, jogged in ignorance of her true identity. Now, without a cap and sunglasses, it was time to see if recognition would spark in their eyes.

"Global Runners… Go!" Patricio shouted.

The starting call unleashed the group like a river breaking through a dam. The leaders surged forward while the middle runners set off at a measured pace, and those at the back began their uphill battle with a steady walk.

Jenn shadowed Karen, her strides easy and unhindered by the thin air. But as the incline steepened, the veterinarian's pace waned, and Jenn seized the moment to pull up alongside her.

"Be careful if you're not used to the elevation. We don't need anyone to faint on the first day," Jenn advised. She made sure her voice was even and firm.

Karen, grappling with the thin air, managed a nod and a strained, "Thanks." A moment passed before recognition sparked in her eyes. "Wait—your name?"

Jenn leaned into the moment; her voice low, she answered, "Detective Jenn Moreno. We've spoken before. You know, the syringes?"

Karen skidded to a halt, her eyes wide with sudden understanding. "Oh, my God! It is you. I thought you looked familiar." The words tumbled out between labored breaths. Jenn waited patiently as Karen processed the revelation. "Why are you here? I haven't done anything. I didn't even know the oil guy was in the hotel," Karen stammered, her defenses rising around her like the hackles on a dog.

"Of course not. But my investigation isn't finished, and since everyone was heading out of town, I needed to come along," Jen explained, pausing to let her words take effect. She then added a chilling afterthought, "Also, it's probably best not to mention to the others that you're a potential murder suspect."

Karen's face lost color, even under the harsh Andean sun. "No, I'm not—I mean, I won't tell. What do you expect me to do?"

"Simple. Keep my identity a secret from the rest. Can you manage that?"

"I can. My lips are sealed." Karen pressed a finger across her mouth. "Honestly, the supplies are meant for animals in need, not people."

"Good. Not a word." With that, Jen dashed up the trail, leaving Karen to her solitary walk.

The investigation was progressing more smoothly than Jen had expected. She overtook a few runners from the middle pack, setting her sights on Christie Adams. The woman was alone—perfect for another discreet chat.

"Christie! How's the run?" Jen called out.

Without slowing, Christie replied, "Not bad. I'm used to running hills, but this altitude is something else."

"Take a moment to admire the crater on your left," Jen suggested. "It's a sight to behold."

Christie glanced over and was awe-struck. "Incredible! I never imagined we'd experience this."

They stood atop the ridge of an ancient, lush volcano. Its crater, now a serene lake, was cradled by greenery, a tranquil heart in an equatorial paradise. The trail they were on, maintained by the park service, skirted the rim. The route chosen for their run was a twelve-kilometer loop around the ancient volcano.

"Not many extinct volcanoes back in Minnesota, huh?" Jen quipped.

"None at all," Christie responded, then eyed Jen suspiciously. "How did you know I'm from Minnesota?"

"And that your husband is an engineer with ties to Aspire Oil?" Jen pressed on.

Christie's memory raced back to the previous night's hotel encounter. "You're the detective. What are you doing here?"

"Merely continuing my investigation, even though everyone suddenly took off," Jen explained.

"We're just following GR's travel itinerary," Christie countered.

"Sure, but remember, you and Joe know who I am. The others don't. Let's keep it that way," Jen urged.

"Why should I?"

"It complicates my job. Plus, do you want everyone to know you were one of the prime suspects? And perhaps still are."

The standoff between the two women was palpable. Christie was incensed at being suspected and cornered. Yet, she knew that legal complications in a foreign land could be dire, as she had seen in countless movies.

Christie finally broke the silence. "All right! But this is the last time we speak. And drop the murder threats."

"Agreed. Please relay this request to Joe as well."

"Done!"

They resumed their run without another word. Jen, feeling a surge of victory, picked up her pace, leaving her suspect trailing behind. Ahead, she heard a sharp "thunk," followed by an expletive. Around the bend, one tourist was on the ground beneath a viewing sign. He was being tended to by another runner.

Not my job, Jen thought, picking up speed. She had time to recover if she wanted to place in the top ten — or better.

CHAPTER 9

ARMY OF ONE

As Jenn surged forward on the rugged trail, her breath came in steady bursts, matching the rhythmic pounding of her shoes against the rocky path. The high altitude of the Andean foothills was her natural environment, but her eyes were fixed on the figure ahead—a towering man whose muscles flexed with each stride.

"You are very fast for a big man, Señor." Jenn remarked, her voice steady despite the exertion as she caught up to Jarrod Turner.

"Thanks. Lots of training," he replied, a grin breaking across his face as he glanced at her. "You're pretty fast yourself, for a snack vendor. Clearly, you're a trained runner."

"I grew up around here. I'm used to the altitude and the terrain." Jenn eyed him speculatively. "You've been through some pretty serious training to do this. Were you military?"

"Yep. Army, twelve years."

"My father was Ecuadorian Army. Were you infantry, artillery, air defense, or something else?"

"Army Ranger, so a master of all trades."

"My dad says a Ranger knows hand-to-hand combat, sniper skills, explosives, infiltration, and sneaky ninja stuff. Is that right?"

"Your father is well-informed. Did he ever train with us?"

"I think so, but he was very secretive about those things."

"Understandable." The conversation and the steep incline challenged their breathing, which made talking difficult.

Jenn slowed her pace slightly. "I'm going to drop back a little. I need to catch my breath."

"Good talking to you. See you at the finish." With a nod, he surged ahead, leaving Jenn to ponder her next move.

As she watched him pull away, Jenn considered the implications. A trained soldier could certainly execute the precise and deadly actions required to kill someone as well-known as Ortega leaving no evidence behind. She made a mental note to add these details to her notebook when she was back on the bus.

Jenn kept a steady pace as she neared the end of the race. Scanning the horizon, she estimated her position—likely only four runners ahead of her. Finishing strong would honor her Ecuadorian roots and still maintain her cover with the Global Runners.

Descending the last hill, the finish line came into view, marked by vibrant flags fluttering in the brisk mountain breeze. Patricio, her colleague, was already waiting at the snack table, his face lighting up with a broad smile and an enthusiastic thumbs-up.

"Jenn, apparently, you're more runner than tour guide," Patricio greeted her as she approached. She was panting slightly, but smiling.

"I do all right," she replied, pride flickering in her eyes. Together, they busied themselves replenishing the drinks and snacks while waiting for the rest of the group to finish, too.

While they worked, Jenn took a moment to text her boss, Castillo. "Chief, has the medical examiner determined the cause of death yet? It would be a big help if I knew what I was looking for out here."

The response wasn't immediate, but it eventually came. "Inconclusive. Possibly poison. Or strangulation. Or blunt force to the chest. The medical examiner says there are vague signs of all three."

"Not helpful," she typed back, frustration evident in her brief reply.

"Tell me about it. Btw, where are you?"

"Still hanging with the tourists. I got a temp job as part of the guide team. Good undercover."

"Hanging where?"

"We're at some nature preserve outside the city. Not sure exactly where." Jenn's response was deliberately vague, buying her time to continue her investigation.

"Stay in touch," Castillo replied succinctly.

As Jenn considered the ambiguous medical findings—poison, strangulation, blunt force—she realized any of the tourists could still be suspects. She quickly packed away the last of the snacks and joined the others as they piled onto the bus.

Finding her usual seat taken, she spotted an empty one near the front and settled just as the bus began to roll. Allen, the Argentine she had met earlier, was in the adjacent seat.

"Chica, where have you been? I was afraid another rock had run over you," Allen joked, attempting to lighten the mood.

"You didn't see me because I was so far ahead of you on the trail," Jenn retorted, her smile sharp rather than friendly.

"I will keep an eye out for you at the next one," Allen murmured, lowering his voice. "We don't want to lose the nosy detective." Then he winked in a smug, condescending way.

"You just keep that to yourself." Jenn's tone was firm, her eyes narrowing. It was not a suggestion, but rather a command.

"Sí," Allen replied, turning his gaze to the window to avoid further confrontation.

The rest of the journey was filled with chatter from the other tourists, but Jenn and Allen sat in a tense silence. When the bus finally pulled into the old hacienda hotel, nostalgia mixed with Jenn's professional focus. The place reminded her of her college vacations, complete with a pool, hot tub, billiards, and even a clandestine cockfighting ring for those aware of its schedule. She knew such activities weren't part of the itinerary for the American visitors.

Zuri, their tour leader, stood and announced the evening's schedule with a cheerful tone. "Happy hour at six. Dinner at seven. Everyone, get your room key from the front desk."

As the group began the usual shuffle to disembark, Jenn's thoughts lingered on her investigation. Each piece of conversation, each interaction, now felt like a clue in the sprawling puzzle she was determined to solve.

68

CHAPTER 10

UNFORESEEN PARTNERSHIPS

The lobby of the rustic hacienda, nestled high in the Andes, buzzed with the arrival of its guests for the evening. Jenn Moreno stood in line, her thoughts wandering, until the hotel clerk's voice snapped her back to reality.

"Jenn Moreno, here you are, room 201," said the desk attendant, handing her a key without sparing her another glance.

Until then, it hadn't occurred to her that she was a last-minute replacement for a male guide. So, he was probably paired with another man. "Umm, who's my roommate?" Jenn inquired, trying to mask her anxiety.

From behind, a cheerful voice responded, "I am."

Turning around, Jenn was greeted by Zuri, who was playfully brandishing a matching key. The relief on Jenn's face was palpable, though tinged with concern. "Oh, thank you, Zuri. But I don't want to impose on you. I thought you'd have a room to yourself."

Zuri's laughter filled the air. "Usually not. I typically share a room with Sheryl, the other event director. We spend half the night working out the latest kinks in the plan. But she couldn't make it this time, so there's an empty bed."

"Or it was until the original guide canceled and I was sent as his replacement," Jenn admitted, still uncomfortable about the arrangement.

"No problem at all. I'm used to it, but you might have to help me with some planning instead of sleeping." Zuri winked.

"Happy to help. Being part of this trip is an enormous privilege for me. Just tell me what you need."

"Right now, let's drop off our luggage because happy hour starts in fifteen minutes. We don't want to miss that," Zuri said, already heading toward their room with purpose. Jenn quickly followed, excited about the potential insights this new partnership could provide.

Within minutes, they found themselves in the bustling courtyard bar; the air was filled with the scent of exotic drinks and the sound of lively chatter. Jenn, eager to enjoy the local culture, decided on a regional specialty for their drinks.

"Dos canelazo de Imbabura, señor," she ordered confidently from the bartender.

Zuri, intrigued, asked, "What's that? I've never heard of it."

"It's a traditional drink here in the highlands, made from aguardiente and local root plants. It's quite unique — not as polished as commercial liquors, but it's full of local character," Jenn explained.

"I'm game," Zuri said, taking a tentative sip before reacting to the strong flavor. "Definitely not smooth. It's got a fruity, rooty kick to it."

Jenn nodded. "This area is the only place they make it like this. The lowlands try, but they can't match the altitude or the dry air here for fermentation."

"You call this dry? I've been sweating non-stop." Zuri laughed, fanning herself.

Jenn laughed, too, before ordering another round. Now was her chance to learn more about the Global Runners. "Zuri, you're from England, but you work with this American company out of Colorado. How did that happen?"

"Actually, I'm from Wales," Zuri corrected gently. "Most people outside the U.K. aren't very familiar with it. But I used to guide tours in Spain and France. Then I met Sheryl on a scouting trip, and by the end of the night, I was working for her. Now, I lead trips all over the world."

Jenn marveled at the idea of such an adventurous career, contrasting sharply with her own routine of chasing down the same crimes in a big city year after year. "That sounds way more exciting than my job at the water department."

"See, you're making your way up. Just being here is a step forward. You could be stuck in an office right now," Zuri encouraged.

Jenn, scanning the crowd, mused on the challenges of managing such a diverse group. "How do you handle all these ruffians?"

"They're mostly fantastic, really. Some have become close friends." Zuri pointed out Samara across the bar. "She's been on ten trips with me. We're practically family now. When she's in the U.K., she stays with me, and I have a place to crash at her house in California."

As the evening wore on and canelazos flowed, Jenn's attention drifted momentarily. She snapped back just as Zuri was discussing a couple who had been desperate to join the trip.

"They were persistent, checking daily for cancellations since we were at full capacity for the Galápagos," Zuri explained.

"That sounds intense. Couldn't they have just waited for the next trip?" Jenn pondered, her detective instincts tingling.

"They said it was now or never because of schedule conflicts." Zuri shrugged.

Just then, with the effects of the canelazo sharpening her focus, Jenn realized the importance of this detail. "I'm sorry, who were the last-minute additions again?"

Zuri was feeling the effects as well. "Those two! Alice and Cathy. Let's go talk to them." She began pulling her roommate toward a table full of people.

When they arrived at the table, she pointed. "Alice got the very last seat on this trip. She couldn't wait six months for the next one. Had to be now. I forgot the reason. What was the reason again, Alice?"

"I'm moving to a new job. I won't have any vacation time built up when I start."

"Yes, that's right. No vacation time. Alice, we pulled it off, didn't we? Here you are." Zuri waved her arms in the air to encompass all of Ecuador.

Alice was enjoying the happy hour as well. "And it has been amazing so far. Very successful trip. I got all my work done in Quito, so now I'm free to enjoy the wilderness."

"Work? You were working? No work on a Global trip. Only running and relaxation," Zuri scolded playfully.

Alice answered, "Some jobs can only be done in a specific place at a specific time." She pointed her fingers at Zuri like they were pistols and made a gunshot sound. Then she burst into laughter.

Jenn stored away every detail. Their urgency to be on this trip struck a chord with her. The night was drawing to a close, but her mind was just getting started. Tomorrow, she would follow up on this new lead. For now, she and Zuri agreed to call it a night, retreating to their room filled with newfound camaraderie.

CHAPTER 11

DARK SUSPICIONS

As the darkness deepened, casting long shadows across the landscape, the day's vibrant activities—happy hour, dinner, and yet another round of cocktails—gradually wound down at the hacienda hotel nestled in the lush outskirts of Ibarra. Most guests, like Zuri, had succumbed to the lull of sleep, their adventures paused until dawn. However, Jenn, fueled by a restless urgency, ventured silently onto the moonlit pool deck, her phone in hand, needing to share her findings with a colleague.

Her voice was a whisper against the soft chirping of the nocturnal wildlife. "Carlos, I need to know what's happening in Quito."

Carlos's voice crackled through the other side of the line, tinged with confusion. "What do you mean by 'back in Quito?' Aren't you here, too?"

"I'm working undercover with the running group. They left town, so I had to go, too."

"Wait, does Captain Castillo know about this?"

"He gave me clearance to keep investigating them, so that's what I'm doing. He doesn't need more details, and don't you tell him, either."

"Where are you?" Carlos asked.

"A hacienda hotel near Ibarra. Actually, right now, I'm at the pool trying not to wake anyone," Jenn confided.

"Sorry I asked. Fine, I won't tell him. You wanted to know about the federales' case. They put Delgado, the oil executive, on house arrest. He and his family can't leave their compound. His guards are in jail awaiting bail. The feds are guarding his hacienda gates now."

"Were any of those items they took linked to the murder?"

"Funny you should ask. The darts for the blowgun were tipped with poison. The Shuar people considered it a sign of respect to give him a fully lethal weapon. The medical examiner is testing the poison to see if it matches anything in the victim's blood analysis."

"Has the ME been any more specific about the cause of death?"

"Oh, yes, he has. He says he is definitely positive that the victim was poisoned, choked, and punched in the chest. However, he can't determine which one happened first or which one actually killed him."

Though she had heard the news before, the lack of clarification of what exactly had happened exasperated her. "You've got to be kidding me. How dead did he have to be before the killer was satisfied?"

"I know. But Castillo is thrilled. If we solve this one, he's already planning his speech at the next law enforcement conference."

"And do the feds have any more suspects?"

"They're interviewing people at the local Aspire offices and the warehouse. They're sending a team to the compound in the Amazon where the drilling's going to be done. They're trying to follow the path of the explosives from the airport."

Jenn rolled her eyes. "So, they're sticking with the theory that it's an inside job?"

"Definitely."

"Well, I think they're wrong. Someone in this runner group is involved. You saw that pin with the Ecuadorian flag on it. All these runners have one of those…well, all but one of them do. It's a custom item for this trip."

"Yeah, I remember. But aren't they just a bunch of tourists?"

"Shhh!" Jenn's voice dropped to an urgent hush as she heard a rustling in the shadows at the far end of the pool. She paused, listening intently. More rustling followed, then a small, dark animal darted from the underbrush and scampered along the edge of the building. "Just a rat."

Carlos chuckled. "Or a guinea pig."

She nodded, even though he couldn't see her. "Yeah, maybe." Jenn continued by adding, "So, this group is not as innocent as they all seem. Everyone I talk to has some connection to Aspire." Jenn recounted the suspect list scribbled in her notebook, her voice a mix of frustration and resolve. "I've got Karen Von-something, the veterinarian who's carrying drugs with her on vacation. Then Joe and Christie Adams. He's an engineer for an Aspire supplier. Allen Shur, the Argentine, he's actually the trip photographer. But he's acting very suspicious; either flirting with me or trying to kill me."

Carlos interrupted, concerned. "Kill you! How? What happened?"

"I'll tell you later. Let's stick to my suspect list. Toni and Lisa are a pair of New York lawyers working for multiple oil companies. Jarrod is a former Army Ranger with the skills and muscle to punch someone to death. And finally, I just met Alice, who begged her way onto this trip at the last minute. She's all giddy about wrapping up a work project before we left Quito and was joking around by pretending to shoot someone."

Carlos whistled, clearly astonished at all she had discovered. "That's quite a list. Have you met anyone who's *not* a suspect?"

"Oh, sure. Patricio, the owner of the guide company. Zuri, who's leading the Americans. Last, there's a couple of accountants from Montana who are more interested in bird watching than anything else."

"Keep your eyes open, Jenn. It sounds like you're in the middle of something bigger than just a group of tourists."

"I know. I'll keep you posted. But for now, I'm going back to my room. It's too creepy out here with just the moon and the sounds of the jungle."

"Stay safe, Jenn. Call me anytime."

"Will do. Goodnight, Carlos."

With the phone call concluded, Jenn stood still for a moment longer, letting the darkness of the night envelop her. She felt the weight of solitude in her mission, an eerie reminder of the dangers lurking in the shadows. With a deep breath, she turned and made her way back to her room, her mind racing with theories and her heart unsure of whom to trust. Lost in her thoughts, she failed to notice the human shadow blending in with the trees outside her room.

As she closed the door behind her, the four walls welcomed her back to the semblance of safety. Jenn couldn't shake off the feeling that every moment spent uncovering the truth brought her closer to peril, yet she knew this was a path she had to tread. For now, rest was paramount. Tomorrow would bring its own set of challenges and revelations, and she needed to be ready to face them head-on.

CHAPTER 12

ANDEAN TRADITIONS

It was a beautiful morning for exploring the Inca Trail through the Andes mountains. The trail had been used for over 500 years by the Incas after they had conquered this area and taken control from the indigenous peoples. The section this group would traverse began near the local peaks at 12,000 feet of elevation and dropped to 9,000 feet during the eight-mile run.

Jenn was up early and preparing for her duties as the official provider of fuel and hydration for the group. She had organized a special treat for the group—a local brew of guayusa tea, a revitalizing concoction that harked back to the days when Incan couriers ran these same paths. The ancient blend of leaves and roots was more than a beverage; it was a sip of history, energizing and reassuring. Jenn anticipated the invigorating taste, even though she would be serving rather than joining the run.

Zuri was nearly ready to depart as well. As Jenn stepped out of their shared room, the tranquility of the morning was broken. A soft "thump" drew her gaze to the doorframe where a dart, its feathered end quivering, was embedded ominously at shoulder height.

"Aei!" Jenn exclaimed, her instincts kicking in as she dove for cover. The wooden porch railing and the thick brush around it provided protection as another dart sliced through the air, its intent deadly.

Hearing the commotion, Zuri appeared at the door with her suitcase in hand, concern etched across her face. "What's wrong?" she asked, spotting Jenn laying on the ground.

"Get back inside. Poison dart," Jenn barked, her voice sharp with urgency.

Zuri, unfamiliar with such dangers but acutely aware of the word "poison," quickly retreated as another dart thudded into the sturdy wood of the door.

"Jenn, are you okay?" Zuri's voice trembled from behind the safety of the closed door.

"I'm fine. Stay there. I'm going to check it out," Jenn replied, and she kept her voice calm, despite the adrenaline surging through her veins.

She crawled to a larger bush, cautiously rising to her knees to survey the area. The compound was still; the gardens seemed to be frozen in time, and the morning light revealed little in the shadows. In a crouch, she moved from cover to cover, always watching for movement and fearing a dart to an exposed arm or shoulder. But whoever had launched these silent attacks had vanished — efficiently, silently, professionally.

Returning to the safety of their room, Jenn knocked and entered. Zuri's eyes were wide with fear. "What happened? Who's out there?"

Trying to ease her friend's fears, Jenn opted for a half-truth. "It was probably just some kids messing around with a blowgun. They accidentally shot this way."

Zuri looked skeptical. "Playing? With a lethal weapon?"

"It's only lethal if the darts are poisoned," Jenn countered, deliberately omitting the genuine danger. "There's no one out there now. It must have been from across the field. They couldn't see us."

"You're sure no one's trying to shoot us?"

"Well, not anymore," Jenn tried to reassure her with a forced smile. "Let's go, or we'll miss the bus."

Once Zuri and their belongings were safely on the bus, Jenn took a moment to send a quick text message: "Carlos, I need you here. Definite threat. Pack a bag. I'll send location and cover details later."

She then sought out Patricio, her race boss. "Patricio, this experience has been incredible. Didn't you mention needing a second photographer, though?"

"That's right. We're short-handed since our second guy dropped out for another gig," Patricio explained.

"I know someone perfect for the role. His work is stunning, especially with action shots and outdoor lighting," Jenn offered, not disclosing that the "action shots" Carlos usually captured were far grimmer than landscapes. Then she added, "And he'd do the job for free if you covered his room and board on the trip."

"Free? That fits our budget. He can join us at the next stop. If his work impresses me, he stays," Patricio agreed.

"Thanks. He'll exceed your expectations," Jenn assured him, masking her relief with a professional smile.

Back on her phone, she confirmed with Carlos: "Congrats! You're in as the new photographer. No pay, just room and board. Meet us in Coca tomorrow night. Bring your gear—and your pistol. You're undercover, remember?"

Before boarding the bus herself, Jenn secured the dart from earlier inside her wallet, a potential clue to the unseen threats lurking on this seemingly idyllic trip. The dart was a silent testament that someone knew precisely why she was here.

BEAR RELAY

As dawn broke, the mountain summit was shrouded in a cool, wet mist, a picture-perfect example of the quintessential morning high in the Andes. The wind carried the fresh, earthy scent of rain-soaked soil. Amidst this pristine setting, the runners gathered, their breath visible in the chilly air, warming themselves with cups of guayusa tea.

Patricio, the race guide, stood before the group, his face alight with enthusiasm, despite the wind. In his hands, he held a black and white stuffed bear, introducing it with a warm smile. "This is Sheryl Bear. She'll be our race mascot," he announced. "The Inca Trail we are about to run was used to send messages across the country by young men called chaskis. They also carried small packages with their messages. Sheryl Bear is our package, and each of you will have a chance to carry her on this journey. The fastest runner will carry her first. After a quarter of a mile, that person will set the bear on the trail for the next runner to pick up. In this way, the mascot will work its way backward through the line until everyone has had a turn at moving her forward. Do you understand?"

The runners, clad in lightweight gear and eager eyes, nodded in agreement, charmed by the idea. Without discussing who would take the bear first, Patricio walked over to Dave and thrust it into his hands.

"Global Runners… Go!" Patricio's voice cut through the crisp morning air.

With that, the runners took off, their steps quick and light as they descended the ancient trail, vanishing into the misty landscape. The sounds of their footsteps were soon swallowed by the vastness of the mountains.

Turning to the two women who had opted out of the race, Patricio remarked, "Señoritas, you will not be running today?"

"Nope. The weather's too cold and the terrain's too rough. We'll ride back down with you," Rachel responded, her voice firm, yet friendly.

"Well, climb aboard. It's a much longer drive than it is a run. They have the shortcut through the mountains," Patricio said before leading them back to the vehicle.

As the bus wound its way down the precarious mountain roads, it became a journey of its own. The narrow, twisting paths demanded careful navigation, causing the bus to sway and bump along. At one point, the driver paused to let the women step out into the fresh air to relieve their queasy stomachs.

When they climbed back onto the bus, Jenn attempted to engage the two in conversation, gathering bits of their life stories over the thrum of the engine. "Where are you both from?" she inquired, seizing the opportunity to learn more about them.

"Minnesota," the woman who Jenn had heard someone refer to as Colleen replied.

"Florida," said the other.

Their conversation meandered through topics from career choices to personal anecdotes, revealing layers of their personalities and backgrounds. Rachel, the former teacher, shared her reasons for leaving her profession, while her new friend from Minnesota discussed the challenges and rewards of running a construction company.

As the bus finally arrived at their destination, they found Dave waiting at the gate of the compound, looking surprisingly fresh and rested. "What took you so long?

I've been here for thirty minutes," he joked, helping to offload supplies from the bus.

With everyone else distracted, Jenn seized the opportunity to conduct her secret mission. She boarded the bus alone, locking the door behind her. Systematically, she searched through all the bags that were left behind, her hands moving with practiced precision. Inside one bag labeled "Karen," she found a vial of insulin—a potentially significant clue, depending on Ortega's cause of death. Joe Adams' bag revealed a newspaper from Quito, its headline screaming about an oil executive's murder, a story Jenn was already very familiar with.

Her search concluded with no dramatic discoveries, but her mind was filled with new suspicions and connections. The knocking on the bus door pulled her back to reality. Alice was waiting outside.

"Sorry, I needed some privacy to change my clothes." Luckily, Jenn hadn't crossed paths with Alice that morning.

"Oh, that's exactly what I was hoping to do. Can you stand guard at the door for me?"

"Sure. No one comes in until you come out." Jenn took up her post on the bus steps. Calling over her shoulder, she asked, "What kind of business were you wrapping up in Quito before we left?"

Alice looked back, so, so startled at the question that she stood frozen for a moment. "Did I say that?"

"Yes, back at the hacienda during happy hour. We were all having such a good time."

Alice paused, trying to remember. Then, she offered, "It was just a payment collection for my client. We had a customer who owed us for past services. He was difficult to reach via email, but he proved to be much more cooperative in person."

"And then you went on vacation?" Jenn asked.

"Sure. I actually got a bonus for doing the job while I was here. Saved the company from sending their own person."

"Business and pleasure mixed into one," Jenn said.

"Exactly." Alice smiled and looked pleased with the memory. "Exactly," she repeated.

After Alice finished changing, both women exited the bus to allow others to get to their bags. Jenn passed Karen on the way out and gave her suspect a knowing look of recognition. She was thinking, *I see you*, and hoped the message carried through her expression.

Jenn's phone emitted an urgent chirping tone. She knew who it was without looking. Stepping away for privacy, she answered, "What's up, Chief?"

"Moreno, we're joining the feds on another raid."

Uh-oh, she thought, as her mind raced for excuses for why she couldn't be there.

Before she could speak, Castillo went on. "We're hitting the Aspire Oil compound outside of Coca."

"What? Where?" Jenn couldn't believe what she was hearing. Did he really need her to go to Coca? The GR group was actually moving to an ecolodge just downriver from the town tonight.

"Coca! Do you know where that is?"

"Well, sure. When do you need me there?"

"Tomorrow. Noon. We're rendezvousing at the local police station. Then we take a boat to the compound."

As Jenn disconnected the call, the entire group was gathering at the finish line for a wild celebration. Steve was the last runner in the group today, and he strode confidently toward the finish line, waving Sheryl Bear over his head. He was the final chaski delivering the important package to its destination.

A FEAST OF UNITY

With the daily race finished, it was time to move on to an important cultural experience for the day. Patricio and his team radiated pride as they introduced the special activity, which was steeped in cultural immersion and tradition. The morning had started with the stimulating brew of guayusa tea along the mystical stretches of the Inca Trail. Now, as the morning gave way to afternoon, they were about to delve into the heart of Incan hospitality with a traditional pamba mesa meal in a quaint farming community nestled in the lush, rolling hills.

The journey there was filled with anticipation. None of the Americans, who were admittedly diverse in their backgrounds and bursting with curiosity, had encountered anything quite like this before. They clambered off the bus as it shuddered to a halt on a dusty road bordered by fields of golden maize and emerald quinoa.

Patricio, their guide and bridge to this ancient world, gathered the group under the shade of a sprawling ceibo tree. "Today, we are guests at a pamba mesa, a communal meal that is the very spirit of sharing and community here," he explained, his voice brimming with reverence. "Such meals are pivotal during festivals, family milestones, or following a minga."

Jarrod, his brows knitted in curiosity, interjected, "Minga?"

"Oh, apologies." Patricio chuckled lightly. "Mingas are a community construction project. Everyone comes together to contribute their labor toward building a public facility like a school or grain storage. Or we might also use a minga to rebuild a family's home after a disaster."

Stella, connecting it to a familiar concept, added, "Like an Amish barn raising?"

Patricio, unfamiliar with the Amish, nodded appreciatively as Jenn, who had explored the Amish country in Pennsylvania, elaborated, "Similar intent, but the cultural and spiritual nuances here are different."

As they walked toward the heart of the village, Patricio continued, "Typically, a white cloth is spread on the ground. Then, participants bring the food they are able to share, and each person adds their dish to the cloth. Once the food is ready, everyone sits along the cloth and uses their hands to eat, rather than utensils and dishes. But, for our group, they've brought along dishes."

The communal space was a vibrant tableau. Large, flat stones served as tables, laden with an array of dishes that painted a vivid picture of the local agriculture and culinary practices. At least two dozen families had contributed, creating a mosaic of colors and scents that tantalized the senses.

Stella, overwhelmed by the display, whispered to Patricio, "This is truly impressive. I feel so privileged."

The villagers, dressed in a tapestry of traditional attire, stood in a respectful semi-circle. The women wore beautifully embroidered blouses over dark skirts. The distinction between married and single was subtly marked by the presence or absence of a fedora hat adorned with a feather.

A hush fell over the group as a community leader began explaining the feast laid out before them. "Here we have mote, potatoes, quinoa, oca, carrots, and fava beans," he said, pointing at each plate with a practiced hand. He moved gracefully along the array of dishes, explaining each one with pride. "For meats, we have prepared chicken and pork. Sometimes, we include cuy, but today, we thought otherwise." His eyes twinkled with mischief at the mention of the traditional roasted guinea pig. At the end of the table, the host pointed to watermelon, papaya, and mango. Then, he proudly pronounced, "Quimbolitos, for dessert." Noticing that he'd used an unfamiliar word again, he explained, "It is a steamed, sweet pastry baked inside a plantain leaf." He took one and peeled back the leaf to show the sweetbread inside.

With the tour of the dishes concluded, the leader performed a solemn offering. He filled a plate, murmured a prayer in the native Quechua language, and then deposited the food into a small, pre-dug hole in the earth. Another villager promptly covered it with soil.

"This plate is an offering to Pachamama," Patricio translated, noting the curious glances. "A gesture of gratitude for the abundance provided and shared."

The group had heard many references to the Earth Mother, Pachamama, in their short time in Ecuador and were familiar with her Incan identity as the primary goddess figure of the people. She was also an ever-present and independent deity with the creative power to sustain life on Earth. Her shrines were hallowed rocks or the boles of legendary trees.

The ceremonial offering broke the initial reserve of the visitors, who, led by Patricio, explored the feast with a respectful eagerness. Questions and conversations blossomed, bridging cultures over shared plates.

Stella, gesturing toward the robust structure of the nearby meeting house, inquired, "Was this building a minga project?"

"Yes," replied the same host who had described the food. "It was a significant undertaking, supported by many pamba mesas. It is a symbol of the blessings of Pachamama and the strength of our community."

Their host then held out a cup of dark yellow liquid. "Try this."

"Um, what is it? I am allergic to many foods," Stella said.

Stepping up, Dave took the cup, explaining, "I'm not allergic to anything. But, yeah, what is it?"

"This is chicha de jora. A mild drink," said the host.

Patricio explained, "Chicha de jora is a corn beer created by germinating maize, then extracting the malt sugars and boiling the wort. Then, it ferments in those large, earthen vats over there." He pointed to large clay vessels sitting under a thatched roof. "The process is like the brewing of European beer. Here, I think they add some quinoa to give it body, before boiling it down with chancaca, or cane sugar."

Smacking his lips after a healthy sip, Dave proclaimed, "Definitely corn. Sweet. Light taste of alcohol, but not like a traditional American beer."

After his assessment, several others were eager to try a glass of the concoction.

As they ate, the Americans got up the courage to ask questions about the community, the culture, and the traditions. They found the young women to be the most eager to talk to outsiders, sharing their secrets and asking for similar details from their guests.

Eva commented to a young woman, "I noticed that everyone's hair is braided down the back. It's beautiful. Is it the style or a sign of being single?"

"It is a sign of respect for the traditions of our people. It says we are one with our ancestors and we remember who they are. It is also a law in traditional Incan communities that all women wear this braid."

Standing outside the primary group, Jenn watched everything with approval. She had attended similar meals with her extended family and knew the significance of sharing food in this way. She was pleased at the respect and the sense of privilege the Americans were showing toward the community and the meal. For a few hours at least, she stopped looking for a murder suspect in the crowd. Today was about connection, about the shared human experience nurtured under the watchful gaze of Pachamama, whose presence was as palpable as the earth beneath their feet.

CHAPTER 15

OIL AND WATER

Zuri commanded the undivided attention of her audience. With a charismatic tone, she announced, "I hope you all cherished the vistas of the Andean highlands. Now, brace yourselves as we embark on the next chapter of our expedition: the mystic Amazon rainforest."

A wave of enthusiastic cheers echoed among the runners; their excitement palpable in the crisp air.

"The transition will be stark," Zuri continued, her voice reflecting the seriousness of their journey ahead. "We'll descend from the breathless heights of 10,000 feet to just 1,000 feet above sea level. Prepare to swap the chilly winds for a cloak of humidity and heat each morning."

"At least it'll be easier to breathe," quipped Stella, trying to find a silver lining.

"True, but it'll be fifty percent water that you're breathing," Zuri replied with a wry smile.

Global Runners had the moving routine down to a science. Luggage was compactly stored, and each runner had their essentials in a day bag. The schedule for the day was crystal clear to all.

Their flight landed at the quaint Coca airport, which boasted just two gates. Each "gate" was nothing more than a doorway leading from the tarmac into a small, sweltering terminal building devoid of air conditioning. Stepping off the plane, the group instantly felt the tropical embrace of the Amazon. The temperature and humidity levels were both flirting with the nineties. The layered attire from the highlands was quickly discarded for more suitable, airy clothing.

Amid the hustle, Jenn located Patricio. "I've arranged to meet the new photographer here. His flight's delayed by an hour. I think I'll hang back and come to the eco-lodge later this evening. Is that okay?"

"Sure, we'll manage without you for a bit. You've got the directions to the lodge?" Patricio inquired, masking his concern for her with a casual tone.

"All set. I've already booked a boat for the journey," Jenn confirmed, and in doing so, she used the same confident tone she regularly used in her true role as a law enforcement agent.

"All right, then. See you at dinner for the planning meeting," Patricio concluded and nodded in agreement.

"We'll both be there," Jenn reassured him as they parted ways.

The running group then made their way to the docks, where boats waited to transport them deep into the heart of the Amazon. The two-hour journey promised a transformation from the familiar trappings of civilization to the untamed wilderness of one of the planet's most preserved rainforests.

Once they were gone, Jenn hailed a taxi for an equally exciting trip to the local policia station, where she would meet with the federale task force.

With her badge clearly visible, she wasn't interrupted as she strode through the doors of the station and proceeded to the back meeting rooms. Policia stations, like most business offices, were laid out the same. If you knew one of them, you knew the rest.

"Moreno, this way!" Captain Adriane Castillo called out as she entered.

"Are the feds already here?" Jenn inquired, while scanning the room.

"They're outside, prepping equipment. And they've brought a dog," Castillo informed her, his tone laced with a mix of amusement and disdain.

"Which specialty? Drugs, cadavers, explosives, or just for protection?" Jenn asked as her eyes narrowed slightly.

"Explosives. Seems they're not taking any chances," he replied before handing her a bulletproof vest marked "Coca Policia," a clear sign of its borrowed status.

"Hey, policia! Let's go!" Jenn saw it was the same commander from their earlier mission at the hacienda. As they went through the back doors of the station, she recognized several of the team from the hacienda mission. That was both comforting and alarming. She knew they were tactically very capable. But she also knew they wouldn't hesitate to put her on the front line and then begin shooting.

Jenn and Castillo followed the rest of the team to the docks, where police boats were moored, ready to take them down the river.

As the boat sliced through the waters of a tributary feeding into the vast Amazon, the dense jungle on either side seemed to watch them in silence. Monkeys occasionally peered down from the treetops, and colorful birds like parrots and toucans soared overhead. Jenn appreciated the deceptive calm of the river, knowing full well the dangers that lurked beneath its serene surface.

"So, we're just looking for the explosives? Matching the brand and lot numbers to what they found at the airport?" Jenn asked.

"That's the story that opened the doors," Castillo answered. "But do you think we need all this manpower to read a few labels?"

Jenn smiled. Typical federale style—over the top. "Of course, we're actually there to find anything remotely suspicious and make a big deal of it. Shake them up. Get them to slip up."

Castillo nodded. "That's the plan."

"And why exactly are you and I invited to this party? It's way out of our jurisdiction." Jenn wasn't complaining. She'd been attracted to the police service for exactly this kind of action.

"They probably need some expendables to carry the explosives," Castillo said sarcastically.

"Beats taking petty calls in the city."

"Mmmhmm," Castillo agreed. They lapsed into silence as the boat sped down the river. Jenn melted into the constant thrumming, and the long days she had before finally seemed to catch up to her. Slowly, her eyes drifted shut.

"Moreno!" Castillo's voice snapped her awake.

She turned sharply, following his gaze to the shore, where a foul smell of oil and methane wafted over the water. There, a dock with several enormous barges marked "Aspire" became visible, each loaded with industrial equipment.

As they disembarked, the slick, oil-stained dock made every step precarious. Waiting for them was a portly man dressed in attire too fine for such a rugged setting.

"Welcome, friends! I am Don Julio, the superintendent. We've arranged everything you need for your inspection," he announced, gesturing toward a fleet of mud-splattered Land Rovers. These cars were the reliable workhorses of remote sites all over the world.

The commander wasted no time. "We appreciate your hospitality, señor. We require access to your records, warehouse, and especially the explosive storage vaults."

With a nod, Don Julio led them away from the river and toward the waiting vehicles. "We also have refreshments waiting for you after your long trip." He was playing the consummate host for a friendly visit, and though Jenn had trouble trusting him, he was good at his role.

As they navigated through the maze of metal structures and heavy machinery, Jenn's senses were heightened. She was keenly aware of the many eyes that followed their every move, a mix of curiosity and caution painted on the faces of the workers.

As promised, Don Julio had laid out a spread of coffee, water, and sandwiches. Though the agents had not arrived for a social visit, they eagerly collected handfuls of the food and drink. Jenn was struck by the strange contrast of armed and armored agents participating in a jungle tea party, though she also helped herself to several items. The commander allowed them several minutes to enjoy their bounty, but he was eager to begin the mission they'd been sent on. Finally, he called an end to the social respite and ordered Don Julio to begin the inspection.

The expansive warehouse was their first stop. As the massive doors slid open, the cool shade inside offered a brief respite from the oppressive heat. Rack upon rack of equipment and barrels lined the space, organized with military precision. Don Julio, with a hint of pride, explained, "We maintain a strict inventory system. Everything is accounted for, down to the last bolt."

The federale explosives expert asked, "Could we see where the explosives are stored?" His tone was polite, yet firm.

"Of course, but may I inquire why such interest in that part of our operation?" Don Julio's voice carried a tinge of wariness.

"Just ensuring everything is up to code, especially materials that pose a high risk," the federale replied smoothly, but his eyes scanned Don Julio's face for a reaction.

Don Julio nodded, understanding the stakes. He led them to a separate, heavily fortified building. Inside, cases of explosives were neatly arranged, each with detailed labels and handling instructions.

As the federale specialist began inspecting the materials, Jenn pulled Castillo aside. "Something doesn't feel right. It's too clean, too orderly."

Castillo nodded in agreement. "I noticed that, too. Clearly, they knew we were coming."

"Let's keep our eyes open and see what lies around the edges," Jenn suggested, her instincts telling her that there was more to this setup than met the eye.

Jenn and the team continued their inspection in the records room, where transactions and shipments were logged. Her eyes quickly picked up discrepancies in the paperwork. Dates didn't line up, and quantities fluctuated from one document to the next. The disorder was a sharp contrast to the tidy storage areas they'd seen before.

"Look at this," she pointed out to Castillo, who was reviewing another file. "This shipment of explosives was logged twice, two weeks apart. It's the same batch number."

Castillo looked over at the document, his brow furrowing. "They're laundering supplies, probably skimming off the top for the black market."

Just then, a shout from outside caught their attention. They rushed out to see the explosives specialist standing with a sniffer dog, which was barking incessantly near a seemingly innocuous pile of crates.

"They've hidden something here," the specialist called out and motioned everyone over.

As the crates were carefully moved aside, a hidden trap door was revealed. Upon opening it, they discovered not only additional explosives, but also illegal firearms and more powerful weapons.

Jenn's gaze met Castillo's, a mix of triumph and concern in both their eyes. "We've got them now," she said. Her voice remained steady, despite the adrenaline coursing through her body.

CHAPTER 16

SECRETS UNCOVERED

The air was tense in the clearing where Don Julio now stood, surrounded by federal agents. Their boots encircled the entrance to the hidden bunker.

"Don Julio, how do you explain all these weapons?" The federale commander's voice was stern, his hand gesturing toward the hidden cache.

"Purely defensive. Wild animals. Attacks from rival companies. You know we're all alone out here. We have to protect ourselves," Don Julio responded, his voice steady, despite the accusatory eyes fixed on him.

"I see automatic rifles, mortars, claymores, and grenades. Is that a rocket launcher at the back? It looks to me like you're preparing to go to war. Or maybe you're expecting war to come to you?"

"No, señor. We are just here to drill for the oil… legally." Don Julio emphasized the last word, a reminder of Aspire Oil's contractual agreement with the Ecuadorian government.

The commander's skepticism was palpable. "But if the government were to change its mind, you could hold your claim here with this cache of weapons."

"We would never do that. Besides, these men are laborers, not soldiers. They can't fight a trained army." Don Julio's hand gesture encompassed the nearby compound, a sprawl of makeshift buildings under the harsh, equatorial sun.

"We'll see about that. For now, we're confiscating these weapons." The commander turned to his team. "Secure this site properly and post a guard. No one touches these weapons except us."

"Yes, sir!"

As the commander and Don Julio headed toward the office, the air thick with tension, Jenn and Castillo were momentarily forgotten.

"Well, it looks like the feds were right about Aspire being tied to the airport package. They're so excited to have a national threat like this. I think they'll forget about Ortega's murder," Jenn observed, but she made sure that she kept her voice low.

Castillo chuckled. "Definitely! They couldn't give you his name right now if you asked them."

Jenn nodded, her resolve to find the killer only hardening. "Which means solving the murder is up to us now, and I'm certain the running group is involved somehow. I want to keep working on them."

"I did give you a week. You can get right back on them when we're back in Quito," Castillo agreed.

"Well, I happen to know that they've moved on from Quito. They're at an ecolodge right across the river." Jenn pointed toward the turbid waters of the Amazon feeder. "I've got a boat coming to take me over there today. If that's okay with you?"

Castillo was visibly surprised. "You knew they were going there all along. You planned for it from the beginning."

"I was hoping it would work out," Jenn confirmed.

"All right, you boat over there and join that crazy group, but I want regular reports. And truthful ones from now on."

As they spoke, Jenn received a notification that her boat had arrived. "Gotta go. My boat's here." She handed Castillo the borrowed bulletproof vest and hurried toward the docks.

The boat idled next to the barges, its engine humming softly. "Carlos, you're right on time! We just unlocked an enormous scandal here. I'll tell you all about it on the ride," Jenn greeted her work partner.

Carlos, all smiles, was momentarily distracted by the water slapping against the giant barge, his camera clicking away at the waves. "Just a second. Let me capture this image."

Their conversation flowed as they navigated the perilous river, dodging sandbars, rocks, and the skeletal remains of old vessels. As dusk enveloped the jungle, an orange pillar of fire blazed from the drilling site, a common oil site practice of burning off the methane. It served as a stark contrast against the darkening rainforest canopy.

Upon reaching the ecolodge, hidden just off a small tributary, they bumped into the dock in almost complete darkness. Together, the pair navigated the walkway up to the main building.

"Patricio, this is Carlos. He's a very talented photographer," Jenn introduced the two men to one another.

Patricio summoned Allen, their current Argentine photographer, and soon, all three were engrossed in Carlos's photos on his laptop, oblivious to the surrounding voices.

Jenn wandered into the lodge's communal area, a fusion of dining room, bar, and community space. Her mood was light; she'd had enough of official investigations for one day.

"Zuri, what's the plan for the evening?" Jenn asked her roommate.

Pointing toward the bar, Zuri replied, "Oh, karaoke over there, and one local is teaching card games to that bunch. They're learning cuarenta, el burro, and tute."

Recognizing the games as uniquely Ecuadorian, Jenn smiled. "Do you play?"

"Not yet, but I can learn."

"Yes! You have to learn cuarenta if you're in Ecuador. It's practically a national sport here, second only to football. I'll teach you."

They settled at a table, and Jenn began removing several cards from a well-worn deck. As she shuffled, she explained the rules of cuarenta, a game she'd played since childhood. The sound of laughter from the karaoke and the clinking of glasses created a lively backdrop as they dove into the game.

"Cuarenta is Spanish for the number forty. It refers to the number of points you need to win a chica. Umm, that means like a set. Forty is also the number of cards used to play." She looked to see if Zuri was following. "Two chicas win the game. Or you can win if your first chica is a zapatería. Umm, that means scoring less than ten points. I'll explain how we count points as we play.

When you win the game, that's a mesa. It means a match, like tennis."

Zuri sounded unsure when she said, "Okay, I guess so. What do I do next?"

"You and I are a two-player game. But they're playing a four-person game." She pointed to the group at the next table. "They are two-person teams against each other, like bridge." Then, holding up a handful of chips, she said, "These are the tantos and perros that we use to keep score."

"Perros, like dogs?"

"Yes, exactly. Tanto is one point, perros is ten points." Jenn continued to teach her new pupil the basics of the uniquely Ecuadorian game, including some tactics for beating other players. The evening passed quickly with competitions between the players and serenading from the karaoke corner.

Zuri, picking up the rules quickly, was soon fully engaged with the strategy of the game. Meanwhile, Jenn's mind was only half-present; she was pondering the connections between the running group, Don Julio's oil compound, and the murder of Ortega. The simplicity of the card game was a welcome distraction from the complexity of the investigation.

As they played, Jenn's phone vibrated. She glanced at it and saw a message from Castillo, asking for an update on her whereabouts and findings. She typed a quick reply, assuring him of her safety and promising a more detailed report in the morning.

After a few rounds of cuarenta, Zuri leaned back, chuckling. She had just won her first mesa.

Jenn smiled, pleased to see her friend enjoying herself. "It's more than just a game here. It's a way to connect with people. Speaking of which, what're we doing tomorrow?"

Zuri thought for a moment, like she was considering her words carefully, before answering, "It's a special run. Something different that you can only do in the rainforest."

Jenn's interest was piqued. "A special run? I want to do it."

With a strategy forming for the next day, Jenn called it a night. She needed to be rested for whatever the special run entailed.

As she laid in her bed, with the sounds of the jungle night acting as a lullaby, Jenn couldn't shake the feeling that she was missing a crucial piece of the puzzle. Her thoughts drifted between the faces of the running group, the hidden weapons cache, and the oil company. The link between them was elusive, but Jenn knew it existed.

CHAPTER 17

BEAR TREASURE

"Special run this morning. You're going to get your first taste of the Amazon rainforest. It's a labyrinth of dense greenery, perpetually damp and treacherously muddy. We've carved a narrow trail for you to follow," Patricio announced just as a gentle rain began to fall, punctuating his words. He looked up through the dense canopy, a smile spreading across his face. "Perfectly on cue. It wouldn't be a true Amazon adventure without the rain. Now, pay attention. Along this path, you'll encounter Sheryl Bear seated beside a curious collection of something. I won't tell you what it is just yet. Your task is to take one and carry it to the finish line. Fail to do so, and you won't be counted as an official finisher today. Everyone clear?"

Stella chimed in with a grin. "Yep. Swipe Sheryl's treasure. Bring it back. Got it."

"Global Runners… Go!"

As Patricio's shout echoed through the humid air, the runners burst forward. The swift and agile were at the forefront, slicing through the mist like gazelles, while the slower participants proceeded with deliberate care, inspecting every tree and stone along their path.

The trail through the jungle was a stark contrast to the drier, firmer paths of the highlands. Even the fleet-footed found themselves struggling, their feet slipping out from under them, sending them crashing into the muddy embrace of the Amazon. Today was not a day for personal bests.

Gasping in awe and frustration, Joe remarked, "Looks incredible, but it's as treacherous as hell. You take the lead."

"With pleasure," Rogerio responded with confidence in his voice. "We train in similar forests back in Florida, minus the monkeys." He gestured toward a pair of primates nestled in the branches above them, and the animals were observing the runners with curious eyes. Rogerio and Joe paused briefly, capturing the moment with their phone cameras — the monkeys huddled together against the damp. Resuming their run, their pace was cautious, yet swift.

Entering a deliberately planted grove that resembled an orchard, Rogerio's eyes caught sight of the black and white stuffed bear next to a mysterious heap of dark, rough-textured objects. "Hope that's not animal poop," he joked aloud to anyone within earshot.

As he drew closer, the objects resolved into large, peach-sized nuts with a coarse exterior reminiscent of coconuts. Snatching one up, Rogerio examined it briefly before sprinting ahead, back into the dense jungle.

The mud soon claimed him; a misstep sent him plunging hip-deep into a murky bog. Momentum carried his upper body forward, and he face-planted into the mire, the strange nut flying from his grasp.

"Well, shit!" he exclaimed, extricating himself and beginning a frantic search through the underbrush for his lost treasure.

Moments later, Joe rounded the corner, narrowly avoiding a similar fate, but ultimately retaining his grip on his own nut. Spotting Rogerio knee-deep in the brush, he couldn't help but laugh. "What're you doing in there?"

"I lost my nut," Rogerio grumbled, his voice muffled by foliage.

Joe's laughter filled the air as he continued along the trail.

Meanwhile, Jenn and Tatyana were finding their rhythm in the unfamiliar terrain. "I haven't fallen yet. How about you?" Jenn inquired as mud splattered her legs.

"Just a slip, but I stayed upright," Tatyana responded, showing her mud-caked hands.

Introductions followed, with Jenn revealing her affiliation with the guide company from Quito and Tatyana sharing her background as a pharmaceutical representative from the arid landscapes of Arizona.

"What kind of drugs do you sell?" Jenn asked.

"All kinds. From headaches, to hemorrhoids, to heart attacks."

Their conversation meandered from personal anecdotes to professional interests, interrupted only when they came upon the bear and its pile of mysterious nuts. "What do you have for us, Sheryl?" Tatyana asked playfully.

"That's cool. It's a cacao nut," Jenn identified, recognizing the seeds used to make chocolate.

"So, we just carry it to the end to prove we completed the race?" Tatyana questioned.

Jenn nodded, already speculating about the evening's activities. Their pace slowed as they navigated another boggy section, this time more cautiously, avoiding the dramatic plunges of their predecessors.

Jenn asked, "Did you know there's a veterinarian in the group?"

"Sure, that's Karen," Tatyana confirmed. "We talk about all the latest drugs together."

"So, you sell animal meds, too?"

"I don't, but my company does. Karen wants to know when she can get some of the newest ones." They ran on a little further. Without really thinking about it, Tatyana picked up the conversation. "I think she brought half a pharmacy with her on the trip. She could probably dose every dog in the Amazon at this rate."

Jenn titled her head to the side at Tatyana's tone. "Is that unusual for a vet?"

Nodding, Tatyana answered, "I think so. I certainly didn't bring any sample meds with me on vacation."

Then, as if uncomfortable with the current topic, Tatyana changed the subject. "Did you see the pillar of fire across the river last night?"

Jenn couldn't confess that she had actually been at the oil company site. "Yes, I noticed it as we came in. That's where the oil drills are, isn't it?"

Tatyana nodded. "Aspire Oil is over there destroying your environment. They're going to pollute this river, just like they have others around the world. It's disgusting. I can't believe the Ecuadorian government agreed to let them in."

"It's a lot of money in the economy and for the people." Jenn knew that the country was split on the issue of oil drilling, but those with money and a voice were in favor of it, so it was happening.

Tatyana's eyes narrowed. "Mark my words, in a few years, you'll regret the deal you made with the devil."

The two continued to chat as they navigated the jungle.

At the back of the pack, Rachel and Colleen walked with their phones out, taking pictures of every interesting feature they saw. There was a constant discovery.

"Look, red mushrooms with heads like an upturned tea cap."

"Here's a highway of cutter ants carrying leaves."

"That's a beautiful flower."

"Yellow mushroom."

"Monkey."

"Parrot."

The pair were spotting more flora and fauna than any of the faster runners.

In the middle of the course, the pair caught up to a faster group who were stumped by the section of trail in front of them.

"What's the problem?" Rachel asked.

Toni pointed down the hill and said, "Road's washed out." The dirt trail that had once been a steep downhill grade for the runners in the front of the pack had been transformed by those feet and the rain into an impassable, smooth surface with no good footing.

Rachel contemplated their options. "Looks like a slide to me." She sat in the mud and skooched forward. Gravity did the rest, pulling her down the slick ramp, twisting and turning her body as she went. The others watched until she reached the bottom. Unharmed, she jumped up and proclaimed, "It's fine! Come on down!"

One by one, the collected group sat, slid, and spun their way to the bottom of the hill. The muddy slide became more compact and faster as each person passed until it was a thrill ride for those at the back of the pack.

The faster someone slid, the louder and more raucous the laughter as everyone embraced the adventure they had discovered.

At the finish line, as the runners reconvened, muddy and exhilarated, Zuri took a headcount. "Looks like everyone made it. Who kept their nut?" she asked, scanning the mud-smeared, but grinning, faces before her.

Hands shot up, some clutching the unique nuts they'd preserved through slips, slides, and tumbles. Amid laughter and shared stories of near misses, the camaraderie of the group deepened, bound by the challenge they'd shared.

"Do you know what it is?" Zuri asked.

Several people answered simultaneously, "Cacao."

A few added, "It's what chocolate is made from."

"That's right. And tonight's activity is that each of you is going to make your own little bar of chocolate. So, don't lose it."

Stella laughed and announced, "Except Rogerio. He has to make white chocolate. I saw him throw his nut at the monkeys after we finished the run."

Rogerio stomped into the brush to look for his lost nut again.

CHOCOLATE CLUES

The morning had challenged the runners with a relentless, muddy trail that snaked through the dense underbrush of the rainforest, leaving them splattered and exhausted. After a thorough cleaning of both their gear and themselves, they congregated in the lodge's dining area, a spacious area with rustic, wooden beams and large, open-air windows that offered views of the lush greenery outside. The air was rich with the scent of damp foliage and the promise of lunch.

"If you have finished your meal, you can join me in making your dessert." The chef, a robust man with a beaming smile and hands that had clearly seen decades of kitchen work, stood at the front holding up a dark nut with a flourish. "Everyone brought their cacao nuts?" he asked, his eyes twinkling as he surveyed the group.

Hands rose one by one, each runner displaying their nut, plucked fresh from the forest. The chef's laughter filled the room as he made his announcement. "The first step in making chocolate is to ferment those nuts for one week."

Disappointment quickly washed over the group's faces.

"You can place all your nuts in that empty bowl on the table. We will use them in a few weeks. In exchange, I have these nuts, which have already been fermented and dried. Please, take one each," he instructed, pointing to a large wooden bowl filled with dark, fermented nuts.

Rogerio, a tall, lean man with an ever-present skeptical frown, raised an eyebrow. "So, I could have left my nut in the forest?" His remark sent a ripple of laughter through the group.

Ignoring the interruption, the chef continued, "The second step is to roast the nut for thirty minutes and let it cool for at least six hours. We roasted all these nuts last night. So, they are ready for the third step. You must crack and winnow them, separating the husk and shell from the inner meat—those are called the nibs." He gestured toward a collection of hammers, picks, and stone cutting boards arranged on the table. "You are all athletes. Get to work on your nut. And be very careful not to leave shells in your nibs. It will spoil the chocolate and crack your teeth."

The team set to work, and the air filled with the sounds of cracking shells and laughter as they learned the delicate art of winnowing. After about thirty minutes, when most were finishing up, the chef resumed his instructions.

"Now, your nibs will go into this heated grinder," he said, flipping the switch on a large, rumbling machine. The runners lined up to add their chocolate nibs into the slowly turning grinder.

Nodding approvingly, the chef continued. "We leave them in the grinder until they are a paste that we call a chocolate liquor. This process will take at least twenty-four hours. At first, it will be very gritty, but eventually, it will become a smooth liquid."

Stella, a spirited woman with long hair and a quick smile, groaned in mock frustration. "Oh, not again!" She extended her hand to receive the chef's already prepared chocolate liquor.

"You catch on quick, señorita." The chef chuckled, pouring a small drop into each person's hand. "Now, you must add sugar and emulsifiers, grinding for another twenty-four hours. It is called conching. Taste it. Just a little."

The group's initial reactions were of disgust as they tasted the sweet and bitter mixture, wiping their tongues on their arms and spitting out the remnants.

"We are almost there. The last step is to temper it, so it becomes smooth and the cocoa butter doesn't crystalize. Then, pour it into molds and chill until it's hard."

Stella eyed a cloth-covered station suspiciously. "I'll bet you have some of yesterday's chocolate waiting for us under that cloth."

With a proud grin, the chef whipped off the cloth. "Of course. Please, try some of the delicious chocolate you have made."

"Oh, this is great!" Rachel exclaimed; her delight was echoed by similar compliments from the rest of the group.

"And that, my friends, is how you make superior Ecuadorian chocolate. Please, enjoy as much as you would like," the chef announced, his eyes crinkling with satisfaction.

After indulging in several pieces of rich, homemade chocolate, the group dispersed. Some were eager to explore more of the jungle, while others felt the pull of a well-deserved nap.

Meanwhile, Jenn motioned for Carlos to follow her to her hut for a private call.

"Hello, Chief. Carlos and I are working the runners. Today, I met a Russian pharma rep who said the vet on this trip has a lot of meds with her. She thought it was unusual. She also reminded me that this murder could have been motivated by ecological preservation. Maybe someone doesn't want the oil company here spoiling the rainforest."

"Well, that's just great. More suspects are just what we need. You're going to have to narrow down your list, or you'll be arresting the entire crew by the time you get back to Quito."

"We will. We're working on it." Jenn then shifted the conversation to the oil compound. "Did the feds find out anything more about that stash of weapons?"

"Yes, a great deal. They've been tracing the suppliers from Don Julio's records and messages. Here's something that might help you out. Guess who supplied the explosives for this site?"

Not familiar with explosives companies, Jenn answered with a name she knew from the cartoons, "Umm, Acme?"

"No. Diamond Construction, Inc. Based out of Minneapolis, Minnesota in America. Didn't you tell me you had some runners from there?"

Jenn consulted her notes. "Oh, that's right. Joe and Christie Adams. And he did say that he's an engineer for a supplier to Aspire Oil. I'll bet it's Diamond Construction. I'm going to have another talk with him."

"There you go. You're narrowing your list already." After taking a deep breath, Castillo continued, "But there's more. Don Julio sent a message to some cryptic email address telling someone to pick up a package at the airport on the day your runners arrived. Guess what the locker number was?"

"It's the explosives the feds found!"

"That's right. Someone was supposed to pick those up before the feds found them, but that person didn't show up."

Jenn wove a story to fill in the blanks. "So, you think Joe Adams was supposed to arrive at Quito airport, retrieve the explosives from the locker, and carry them away with him? But to do what? Who or what was he supposed to blow up?"

"We don't know…at least, not yet. The feds are still sifting everything at the oil compound. But it's looking more and more like your runners are deeply involved in something bigger than just one murder."

The trio exchanged more information and agreed to connect the next day.

Jenn looked at Carlos with excitement in her eyes. "Carlos, we have a visit to make to our explosives engineer.

CHAPTER 19

MONKEY BUSINESS

The tension was thick in the humid air of the jungle ecolodge as Jenn confronted the Adams couple. "You failed to mention that your company makes explosives, which it then sells to Aspire Oil," she stated, her voice steady and penetrating.

Joe, less intimidated than during their initial encounter in Quito, retorted defiantly, "You didn't ask about the company. You were investigating a murder in a hotel."

"That was before we found your company's explosives in a locker at the Quito airport. It was from an order sent to Aspire Oil here in the Amazon."

"I'm confused. Are you asking about a murder or lost explosives?" Joe's confusion seemed feigned. "You know, it doesn't matter. I'm here on vacation. Diamond Construction is an enormous company. Go ask them about their lost explosives."

Jenn's gaze didn't waver. "Yes, but you and the explosives showed up at the airport at the same time. Also, we have evidence that someone was supposed to pick up the explosives on the day you arrived. How many explosive engineers do you think arrived in Quito that day?"

"I'm certain the number is more than one, because I didn't do anything. You need to look for someone else."

Christie finally spoke up, her voice icy, "So you have no evidence connecting us to a murder or lost explosives. You have nothing more than coincidence. Unless you come up with something real, you can just leave us alone. You're ruining our vacation."

Jenn knew she was at a disadvantage, particularly in the remote jungle setting of the ecolodge. The lush greenery enveloped the small huts, and wildlife sounds permeated the air, a stark contrast to the heavy accusations being tossed around. "You're right, but these 'coincidences' keep popping up. We'll talk about this some more when we get back to Quito." She left them with this thinly veiled threat, hoping it would unnerve them.

Exiting the Adams' hut, Jenn passed Toni, the sharp-eyed lawyer, and hoped the conversation hadn't reached her ears. As she glanced back, she saw Christie, visibly upset, gesturing for Toni to come inside.

Carlos awaited Jenn outside the hut with his camera slung over his shoulder. "Carlos, I lowered the boom on the Adams. They stood firm, and I had to admit that I was operating on speculation. But I think I put the fear of arrest into their heads. I want you to keep your eye on them… and your camera. You might capture something useful."

"Sure, I can do that. Everyone enjoys being seen in pictures," Carlos replied, eager for any excuse to use his camera. "So, now what?"

"It looks like those explosives are linked to the murder somehow, but there are too many missing pieces still." Jenn flipped through her notebook. "Explosives from Aspire at the airport. Aspire CEO murdered at the hotel. Aspire Oil compound full of weapons. American running group that's curiously close to all of it. Those are pieces of the same puzzle, but they don't fit together yet."

"Can we search their rooms while they're out on a run tomorrow?" Carlos asked.

"Of course we can! But we have to do it without being noticed. I've searched everyone's day bag on the bus already."

"Did you find anything?"

"Just more meds in the vet's bag, nut nothing I didn't expect."

As daylight waned, Carlos suggested, "We still have some free time before dinner. Can we walk the forest loop? I want to take some nature pictures."

"Sure. I need to let off some steam. We have to be back in time for the nightly planning meeting, though. Remember, we're supposed to be part of the staff."

"Taking pictures is my job. This is a working walk for me."

The trail was a vibrant tapestry of massive trees, overhanging vines, and a chorus of avian calls. Carlos, with his keen photographer's eye, pointed out a brightly colored hoatzin bird. "They're usually browner than that. It's rare to see one that bright. You know they actually nest as a commune. One mates and lays a fertilized egg. Then, all of them take turns keeping it warm and fed. That way, it matures faster and is less vulnerable to predators."

"You're a cop. How do you know all that?"

Carlos shook his head and chuckled. "Oh, no. I'm a photographer who happens to be employed by the policia service. Capturing images of this amazing world comes first. Dead bodies and crime scenes are just the venue I get paid for right now."

"So, you'd be happy working for Global Runners like Allen does if you had the chance?"

"Oh, absolutely. Imagine traveling to a different country every month to capture its beauty."

Their naturalist conversation was interrupted by a rustling noise coming from above them. A squirrel monkey, its small body agile and swift, performed a breathtaking leap across the tree canopy.

Jenn whispered, "That was beautiful." No sooner had she finished those few words than another money leapt through space, followed by a third and a fourth. As the detectives watched, more than a dozen monkeys took their turn at the daring leap, each landing safely in the branches on the other side.

Carlos's eye never left his camera, capturing every one of the daredevils in flight.

The two continued to wait in silence, but the parade of flying monkeys had passed. Finally, Jenn said, "I think I counted fourteen of them. That was amazing!"

"It was a family of squirrel monkeys, and I got it all with my camera. I'll show these to Patricio and Allen at the meeting. They'll probably offer me a permanent job on the spot. It's been nice working with you." He smiled at Jenn, imagining the countries he would soon visit.

"The meeting! We've got to get back. Don't want to get you fired before you're even hired."

The staff meeting convened over dinner. As they discussed the plans for the next day, Jenn glanced across the room at the runners. She noticed that Joe and Christie were sharing a table with Toni and her sister, Lisa. As they talked, each of them cast angry glances at the detective. Jenn guessed that her secret had spread to the pair of traveling lawyers.

CHAPTER 20

TALENT FOR HIRE

"Today, we have another run through the jungle planned." Patricio's voice cut through the morning humidity as the group gathered together, and anticipation buzzed in the air. "Yesterday, you dipped your toe. Today, you'll take a bigger bite."

Stella chimed in, her tone playful, "And you mean that literally. We're going down face-first."

Laughter erupted among the group, easing some of the tension. Patricio grinned. "Today, we'll be higher up from the river. So, it might be a bit drier and less boggy.

But remember, this is the rainforest, so no promises." He quickly briefed them on the course's twists and turns before signaling them to start.

"Global runners… Go!"

Conditioned like Pavlov's dogs, the runners burst into a sprint, vanishing into the dense foliage of the jungle trail.

Jenn watched this banter with envy. She wished she could join the runners today as well. She coordinated logistics while Carlos, with his camera in hand, positioned himself along the course to capture the action.

"Patricio, I've set up the snacks and drinks at the finish. What else do you need?" Jenn asked, eager to contribute more than she had the previous day.

Just as she spoke, the afternoon rain began—a daily ritual here. "Could you set up an awning over the snack table?" Patricio suggested while making his own preparations for the inevitable downpour.

"Yes, Chief!" Jenn replied with a salute, immediately regretting the formal gesture that she often used jokingly with Captain Castillo, her actual boss.

Patricio chuckled. "They'll be a lot muddier today, though they don't know it yet. The course is nearly six miles—uphill, downhill, and zigzagging through the thick forest. It'll be a surprise." He seemed amused at the prospect of the runners' muddy return.

Jenn nodded. "Dave and Oscar should be the first back, maybe in ninety minutes. Should we wait here in the rain for them?"

"No need. Go back to your hut and stay dry. Just be here in an hour, in case they're quicker than expected."

"Thanks. See you soon," Jenn replied, relieved at the chance to get away. This brief respite was her chance to explore the lodge—a risk for sure, but a necessary one for her investigation.

She began with the most secluded hut belonging to Alice and Cathy from Colorado. From the documents scattered around the place, Jenn learned Alice was a collections consultant—hardly the intimidating type— while Cathy handled PR for the hip-hop band Sugar Strawz. Their belongings revealed little connection to any suspicious activities.

Next, she attempted entry into Joe and Christie Adams' hut, but found the door securely locked. Laughing to herself, she thought, *They're cautious, for good reason.*

In Jarrod Turner's room, which he shared with his wife, Tammy, Jenn discovered typical vacation items alongside a suitcase packed with dive gear and high-performance supplements. More intriguing was a passport under the name Jack Hunter, complete with Jarrod's photo and multiple immigration stamps—a clear forgery—and business cards for "Jack Hunter, Specialty Missions Worldwide."

Snapping photos of the evidence, Jenn quickly covered her tracks and returned to the finish line. With no runners in sight, she checked the website listed on the business card. It described Jack Hunter as a retired Army Ranger now specializing in high-risk security solutions — executive rescue, celebrity protection, delivery of sensitive packages, and covert surveillance.

She texted Castillo the photos and website link, requesting a background check on both identities.

"Am I first?" Dave's voice pulled her back to the moment as he crossed the finish line, covered in mud.

"Yes, Dave. You're the first… as usual," Jenn confirmed before checking her watch. "One hour, eighteen minutes."

"That's decent for a jungle run," Dave boasted, and displayed his mud-caked attire.

Patricio appeared, laughing heartily. "Señor Dave, the jungle seems to have embraced you fully today!"

Shortly after, Oscar and Oliver finished neck and neck, followed by other mud-coated runners. Oliver pointed toward the dock. "There's only one way to clean this off!" Energized, the group dashed to the river, leaping in fully clothed.

As they scrubbed themselves clean in the water, Patricio casually strolled to the edge of the dock. "Gentlemen, do you know what else swims in there with you?" The sudden tension was palpable. The runners looked at each other quizzically.

Clutching his crotch, Oscar blurted out, "The penis fish?"

Laughing, Patricio confirmed with a mischievous grin, "Well, yes, but you face no danger with your shorts on. It's not small enough to get through the material. Your real swimming partners are the piranha that swim in there as well." Patricio waved his hand in their general area.

"I'm out!" Dave declared first, retreating swiftly.

"Don't be a chicken, Dave. They won't bother you unless you're bleeding," Oliver teased, though the group quickly transitioned to a more cautious cleaning session from buckets on the dock.

A group of slower runners walked out of the forest, and they were equally coated in the chocolaty earth. They were exchanging stories about their adventures on the slippery trail. Each had their own description of how they had slipped, slid, and splashed their way to the finish. "I got some of your crashes on video," Toni exclaimed.

Amid the laughter and chaos, Jenn's phone beeped. It was a message from Castillo. Her pulse quickened as she read the text, her excitement mounting with a potential breakthrough.

CHAPTER 21

THE BOY SCOUT

Jarrod Turner pushed open the weathered door of his rustic hut, probably expecting the humid silence of the room, its air thick with the scent of rain-soaked earth. Instead, he found an unexpected guest. A young woman occupied the room's sole chair, her figure relaxed but her eyes sharply observant.

"Umm, hello, Jenn, why are you here? I'm married, you know." Jarrod's voice carried a mixture of nervousness and embarrassment.

"Yes, Jarrod, I know. I've met Tammy. That's not why I'm here." Jenn produced her detective's badge with a practiced flick of her wrist, extending it toward him.

He squinted at the badge, then nodded in recognition. "Quito Policia. That fits perfectly. Your fitness, the way you carry yourself, the questions you ask, and that bulge in your pocket. The pieces fall into place. I had you pegged as former military."

Jenn acknowledged his guess with a nod.

"How can I help you, Officer Moreno?"

"Detective Moreno," she corrected him sharply.

"So, you're investigating a crime? You're undercover a long way from Quito. That's unusual."

"The crime is unusual."

"Which is?" he probed.

"For this conversation, I'm interested in talking to Jack Hunter." She held up the forged passport, letting the implications hang in the humid air between them.

"So, you've discovered my alias… while searching my room, I'm assuming. I'm sure Patricio wouldn't approve of that type of behavior from his staff."

"We can address that after we learn a bit more about why Jack Hunter is in Ecuador." Jenn flicked through her phone, stopping at a specific message. "I have an exchange here with the federales who are investigating a package of explosives found at the Quito airport. They have emails sent by an Aspire Oil supervisor here in Ecuador. Do you know what they say?"

Jarrod, a.k.a. Jack Hunter, paused, his expression unreadable. "Why don't you tell me?" he asked.

"They say that the package that they left at the airport would be picked up by 'the Hunter' last Saturday." Jenn scrutinized him for any tell of nervousness. "When did you arrive in-country, Jack Hunter?"

He smiled thinly. "I believe it was Saturday. But I didn't pick up any package."

"No, you didn't, but you were hired to pick it up and deliver it somewhere. Why didn't you carry through on your assignment?"

Folding his arms, Jarrod Turner answered, "Detective Moreno, you're correct that I was hired to deliver that package. But Jack Hunter is a legitimate business. I don't do illegal shit. Clients often hire me to deliver packages of money, documents, even gold occasionally. But I don't deliver drugs, bombs, or anything else like that. The airport package was clearly a bomb."

"You opened the locker? You saw it?" Jenn asked sharply.

Jarrod nodded. "And I could smell it. I immediately closed the locker without touching it."

"Where were you supposed to deliver it?"

"After I got in-country, I received an address for delivery. It was going to 105 Avenue de Cieba."

"And what were you supposed to do with it there?" she asked.

"Just pitch it over a side garden wall."

Jenn continued, "Who lives at 105 Avenue de Cieba? That's a pretty elite area."

"You could look it up. I did. That's another reason I didn't touch it. It's the home of your government's Minister of the Interior." Turner let the gravity of his words sink in.

Jenn's mind raced at the implications. "You're telling me that Aspire Oil hired you to deliver a bomb to the Minister of the Interior?"

"No. I'm telling you that an anonymous client hired me to deliver an anonymous package from an airport drop point to an unknown location in the city. Typical job. That's the job I accepted. The rest of the details came later." Jarrod set his jaw firmly.

"Okay, so maybe you're one of the good guys. Won't your client wonder why you didn't do the job?"

"Not since the feds found it. I can tell them the site was too hot. Also, that's why I have an alias for these jobs."

"Yes, let's get back to this counterfeit passport." She held up the document. "I'm pretty sure the American government wouldn't approve of this forgery. And I'm certain that Ecuadorian Immigration would have issues as well."

"Have you looked at it really closely? That's not a counterfeit, it's just a fake passport. There's a big legal difference."

"How do you figure?"

"That document is good enough to confirm my identity as Jack Hunter to a client. It's not good enough to get through customs or immigration checks."

"There are certainly several stamps in the back."

"All fake. I have one from the Grand Canyon National Park, another from my local coffee shop, anywhere I see one that's passable." Jarrod smiled at his cleverness.

Jenn examined the stamps as he spoke. They certainly were from a strange assortment of places, and none of them were official government entry points. "Indeed, a unique collection," Jenn replied, her tone including both amusement and skepticism. "But it doesn't change the fact that you were involved in a potentially dangerous mission. What now?"

Then Jarrod became the inquisitor. "Detective, can you tell me why an oil company is trying to eliminate a government official? Especially one who just gave them a big contract?"

Jenn thought about it. "I have no clue." Considering whether to trust this supposed Boy Scout, she decided to test him. "Or why do they have a stockpile of illegal weapons at their oil compound across the river?"

Jarrod raised his eyebrows. "They're not afraid of the monkeys. They're afraid the government will change its mind and try to kick them out of the country. That would cost them billions. It sounds like they'll do anything to keep their contract and their facility."

Jenn stared at him. She considered—since he was a former Army Ranger, current adventurer for hire—this guy might have some experience dealing with situations like this one. But she couldn't give him any more information.

"Can I have that back?" Jarrod pointed at the novelty passport.

Jenn tossed it to him. "Okay. For now, I'll assume you're a Boy Scout, but don't tell anyone who I am. And don't try to run off, either."

Jarrod spread his arms to indicate the nearly impenetrable rainforest that surrounded them. "How? I promise to be on the boat for the next stop on our trip." After a moment of thought, he asked, "Why are you here? You didn't know who I was until today, but you joined our group as soon as we left Quito. You're here to investigate something else."

"You're perceptive, Jack Hunter, but I can't tell you everything." Before he could ask any more questions she couldn't answer, she rose to leave.

"I'll figure it out, Detective Moreno."

"You do that, Hunter. But keep our secret, and I won't bring the feds here to talk to you."

"Deal."

Jenn watched him wake his phone and start typing. She assumed he was looking for news that would explain her presence.

CHAPTER 22

ADVENTURE TIME

Jenn dialed her boss's number, concerned by the weight of the information she'd uncovered. The phone rang a few times before Castillo's voice came through.

"Chief, I just had a conversation with Jack Hunter. He was contracted to retrieve the package at the airport, but he insists he refused the job when he discovered it contained explosives. He claims he only accepts legal assignments," Jenn relayed.

"Should we come pick him up for questioning?" Castillo inquired.

"Global Runners will save you the trouble. There's no way to run away from this camp in the jungle, and tomorrow, the entire group is coming back to Quito," Jenn explained.

"Fine. You keep an eye on him. Make sure he gets back here," Castillo agreed. "Now, if he was supposed to get the package, what was he supposed to do with it?"

"That's where it gets serious," Jenn replied.

"Explosives at the airport are serious enough."

"Well, it gets even more serious. Once he arrived in the country, he received a call instructing him to deliver the package to a specific address and throw it over a garden wall. The address happened to be the residence of Jose Cesar, the Minister of the Interior," Jenn revealed.

"What? You mean the Minister of the Interior for Ecuador?" Castillo exclaimed, clearly taken aback.

"Yes, exactly. That's one reason Hunter backed out of the job. He could see the setup and how he would be framed for the bombing."

"So, let me get this straight. Aspire Oil redirected their own explosives to be dropped off at the airport, and then they hired an American mercenary to blow up a government official?" Castillo's voice was filled with disbelief.

"That's the conclusion I've reached as well," Jenn confirmed.

"But why would they do that? Minister Cesar just approved their drilling operations in the Amazon."

"I'm as puzzled as you are, Chief. It's a much bigger scheme than anything I've dealt with before," Jenn admitted.

"I think it's time we meet with the feds and exchange information. We should find out what they know as well," Castillo suggested. "Since your group is returning tomorrow, I'll schedule a meeting for the afternoon. Excellent work, Moreno."

"Thank you. And Carlos is proving to be valuable as well. He has hundreds of photos of everyone on the trip," Jenn added.

"Stay safe, Moreno. There's a killer among them, even if Hunter isn't the one," Castillo warned.

Jenn felt a sense of validation hearing Castillo acknowledge for the first time that a killer was hiding among the runners.

Leaving her hut, Jenn stepped out into the camp, greeted by an unusual silence. Spotting Zuri relaxing in the expansive lodge, she approached with curiosity.

"Where is everyone?" Jenn inquired.

"They're all out on the river, fishing for our dinner," Zuri replied with a mischievous smile.

"What are they fishing for?" Jenn asked, her eyes widening.

"Piranha, of course," Zuri answered in a playful tone.

Jenn's surprise was evident as she responded, "And you trust the tourists to handle a piranha after they catch it?"

Zuri chuckled and shook her head. "Of course not. Someone would lose a finger. We have local fishermen to take care of that part."

"They're going to need quite a catch to feed this entire crew," Jenn commented skeptically.

"It's symbolic, really. We just hope there's enough for everyone to have a taste. The actual meal is already being prepared," Zuri explained.

Seeking a way to pass the time, Jenn suggested, "Care for a few mesas of cuarenta?"

"Sure, but I warn you, I'm going to beat you this time," Zuri replied, and a smile played on her lips.

The two women engaged in a series of games, and as promised, Zuri emerged as the winner several times.

Jenn's detective instincts got the better of her, and she soon turned the conversation toward their trip and the people involved.

"Do you ever encounter any problems when managing such a large group?" Jenn asked.

"Problems? I could write a book about the problems, but nothing too serious," Zuri replied, reflecting on the experiences they'd encountered.

"All right, tell me a few stories," Jenn encouraged, eager to hear more.

Zuri thought for a moment before a gleam of excitement sparked in her eyes. "Ah, I've got one. You've met Stella, right?"

Jenn nodded, recalling the sociable woman, who seemed to be acquainted with everyone in the group.

"Well, once in Costa Rica, we had a bit of an adventure with Stella. During a jungle run, we somehow managed to lose her. And I don't mean she just veered off the trail and took an extra mile. I mean, she was completely gone. Nobody knew where she had disappeared to," Zuri recounted.

"But clearly, you found her since she's here with us," Jenn interjected.

Zuri grinned. "Yes, indeed. It turns out she took a wrong turn somewhere in the jungle and ended up on a different trail. Instead of descending on our side of the mountain, she unknowingly went down a different face and ended up in the next valley. We were searching for her along the trail. Luckily, she realized she was in real trouble, but she found a road and eventually a truck. With her limited Spanish, she explained her situation to the locals, giving them the name of the park and the trailhead where we had started."

Jenn listened with astonishment, marveling at Stella's resourcefulness and determination.

"The two men in the truck understood her descriptions and, about two hours later, they arrived at our run-site with Stella in the passenger seat. She jumped out of the cab, brimming with smiles and energy, having figured out how to rescue herself," Zuri concluded.

"I can only imagine how relieved you must have been," Jenn commented.

Zuri paused, taking a deep breath. "When I saw her, I burst into tears. The relief and worry I felt suddenly overwhelmed me. It was a stark reminder of the responsibility we carry, guiding tourists through the wilderness of a foreign country. No matter how well we plan, there's always an element of risk involved."

Jenn's curiosity got the better of her, and she couldn't help but ask, "Injuries?"

Zuri chuckled and began retelling some of their past adventures. "Oh, every trip. On our first run here in Ecuador, we had two. Deb took a fall and dislocated her finger. She was all alone, miles away from the finish line. She's a tough one, though. She reset her finger herself, tied it to her healthy fingers, and kept running until she reached the end."

"Dios, Mio!" Jenn exclaimed.

"And then, there was Rogerio," Zuri continued. "He almost knocked himself out by failing to duck low enough under a sign."

Jenn nodded, remembering the incident. "I was there when that happened. I heard the loud 'thunk' and his colorful language. Then, I saw him sitting under the sign, dazed."

"But he got up and finished the race," Zuri added. "And that was just the first day. I'm sure we'll have more mishaps before this trip is over."

Jenn was amazed. "And they keep coming back for more?"

Zuri nodded, a glint of excitement in her eyes. "It's the thrill of the adventure. It's so much more exciting than a week on the beach."

The sound of dozens of voices interrupted their conversation. The piranha hunters burst into the room, their voices filled with excitement as they shared stories about their catch and the one that almost cost someone a finger.

Zuri pointed toward the crowd to emphasize her point. "Adventure."

Carlos, spotting Jenn and Zuri together, rushed over with his camera. "I got some amazing pictures! One piranha leaped out of the water before the bait even touched the surface. I caught it on camera. And then I took some gruesome shots of the guide cutting open a piranha to show us the little fish inside."

Jenn responded sarcastically, "Sounds delicious."

Carlos, missing the joke, innocently replied, "Oh, they clean all that out before cooking them."

Curious, Jenn asked, "So, who caught the biggest fish?"

Carlos grinned mischievously. "That's debatable. Tammy and Barb are still arguing about it."

The lively celebration and fishing stories continued throughout dinner, although only a few of the runners dared to actually try a bite of the carnivorous fish.

As the evening progressed, the post-dinner activities began. People gathered for karaoke, accompanied by generous amounts of drinking. Card games ensued, with a hint of betting involved. The more exhausted members of the group used the ecolodge's Wi-Fi to post pictures of their day's adventures.

Finally, an organized night jungle walk was scheduled to spot nocturnal animals and insects. The participants were instructed not to touch any plants or creatures they encountered. They wouldn't know which were poisonous, venomous, or just plain dangerous.

After the long day, Zuri and Jenn retired to their shared room, preparing their gear for the journey back to civilization. They laid out their clothes and completed their evening cleansing routine. Just as they were about to settle into bed, Zuri screamed at the top of her lungs.

Alarmed, Jenn rushed out of the bathroom, instinctively looking for her pistol. "What is it? Are you okay?"

Zuri, with her back against the wall and her hand over her mouth, pointed at the bed. There, near the pillow, stood a large brown spider.

Jenn recognized it immediately. The Wandering Spider, a creature ingrained in the stories of every Ecuadorian child. "Don't touch it!" Jenn commanded. "It's highly venomous and aggressive."

The creature was six inches across with a hairy brown body and a dark stripe running down its center. As Jenn moved around the room, the spider lifted its front feet and swayed from side-to-side. She quickly assessed the situation, searching the room for something substantial enough to capture or crush the spider. A shoe wouldn't do; she needed something more like a shovel or a frying pan.

Zuri asked, "What should we do?"

"The most important thing is to ensure it doesn't escape," Jenn replied. "We don't want to spend the entire night wondering where it went." Just then, they heard footsteps approaching their door. That was when she remembered something that might help. Jenn stepped outside and grabbed a bamboo pole from the ground, a four-foot-long stick usually used for drying shoes soaked in the jungle.

Jarrod's face was the first to appear at the door, followed by several others. Jenn ordered them to stay back.

She advanced toward the spider, wielding the bamboo pole like a conquistador with a sword. With a swift motion, she brought it crashing down on the bed. Her first attempt missed, but in a flash, the bamboo sword rose and fell repeatedly. Finally, a well-aimed stroke connected, turning the spider into a flat smear on the sheets.

As the tension dissipated, Patricio stepped inside to inspect Jenn's handiwork. "Nice job, exterminator," he commented. Addressing the crowd, he explained, "It was a Wandering Spider, native to the Amazon. They only emerge at night and prefer to wander on the ground in search of prey. They never enter indoor spaces, especially when the lights are on." Glancing at Zuri with concern, he added, "And they're very venomous."

One onlooker asked, "Deadly venomous?"

Patricio nodded gravely. "Sometimes. If bitten, you'll experience cramps, seizures, and a fever. It's an agonizing ordeal, and a few people have died from a single bite." Trying to offer some reassurance, he continued, "But we have anti-venom here at the lodge. It helps."

Jarrod couldn't help but blurt out, "Helps? It doesn't cure it?"

Patricio cursed for letting that tidbit slip. Shaking his head, he admitted, "No, it doesn't eliminate the pain or the fever. You'll still be terribly sick for several days. But at least you won't die." The way he paused at the end of the sentence made it seem that there was supposed to be a "usually" in there somewhere.

Jenn and Patricio took turns providing more details about the spider and assuring the group that it was unlikely for another one to be in their rooms. The spiders were afraid of people, and there were no bugs for them to prey on in the rooms. They also gave instructions for carefully checking the beds, clothes, and shoes for any potential intruders.

In an act of solidarity, Jenn agreed to switch beds with Zuri, but not before changing the sheets. Cautiously, she slid beneath the covers, her mind filled with questions about how the arachnid had found its way into the room and onto the sheets. It was highly unusual, and Jenn couldn't shake off the sense of unease.

FEDERAL AND LOCAL

Upon returning to Quito, Jenn was struck by her changed perception of the city. Once a pulsating heart she felt in sync with, it now seemed like an overwhelming torrent of noise and urgency. The jungle's serene whisper had softened her senses, making the city's relentless rhythm feel like an assault.

After the entire group had settled in, Captain Castillo picked her up at the Hotel Quito, where the entire saga had begun. As they drove, Castillo briefed her, his voice tinged with frustration. "We have a meeting at the federal building in an hour. It took a lot of persuading to get them to agree to take the time. They think they know everything and we know nothing."

Jenn couldn't help but roll her eyes. "Typical. But while they've been chasing an oil company, they totally missed the connection to the runners."

Navigating through the city, Jenn observed the stark contrasts that she had previously become desensitized to. Every building was fortress-like, surrounded by cinder block walls crowned with electrified wire—a stark reminder of the nightly struggle with crime and poverty. By day, Quito masqueraded as a pristine and prosperous city; by night, it revealed a desperate struggle for survival.

"Moreno! Are you with me?" Castillo's voice jolted her from her reverie.

"Sorry, Chief. I'm still adapting to the city's pace. Everything is so much quieter and slower in the jungle."

"I remember. I've got family in Coca, so I get out that way occasionally," Castillo replied, pulling the police vehicle into a reserved spot in the government parking garage.

The elevator hummed softly as it carried them to their destination—a starkly utilitarian conference room where two federal agents awaited. One was a familiar face, Officer Lopez, who had camped out at the policia station; the other introduced himself as Captain Abril.

After exchanging handshakes and pleasantries, all attention shifted to Jenn. She spoke cautiously, omitting sensitive details about Global Runners, and began recounting the events starting from the raid at Aspire Oil's compound. She detailed their subsequent investigation, leading to a suspect at a remote wilderness lodge.

"So, Jack Hunter admits he was hired to deliver a package, but insists he backed out when he saw what it was and received the final delivery instructions," Jenn explained, noting Abril's keen interest.

"Impressive that you figured all this out from a few of Don Julio's emails at the oil compound. However, I think there's more that you're not sharing," Abril remarked, his experience with agency turf wars evident. "But let's continue. What was the delivery address?"

"It was the home of the Minister of the Interior," Jenn paused, letting the gravity of her statement sink in.

Abril and Lopez exchanged glances, a clear sign they were piecing together their own fragmented puzzle.

"You don't seem as surprised as we expected," Castillo interjected. "That means you have reason to believe this makes sense. But the pieces don't fit for us." He was probing for more information.

Abril, deciding to cooperate, explained, "You've given us an important piece of information because it connects a story we've been working on. You're wondering why a company that received an enormous opportunity from our government would try to kill the very official who signed the agreement. Am I right?"

Jenn and Castillo nodded in agreement.

"Our investigation into the connection between Aspire and the government revealed that the minister was canceling the agreement. His office felt that Aspire wasn't living up to their end of the deal," Abril continued.

Castillo voiced the logical conclusion, "So Aspire planned to kill the minister before he could change the agreement? But wouldn't the office just continue the cancellation without him?"

"That all depends on who takes over, what their incentives are, what they've been paid, and by whom," Abril pointed out.

Jenn joined in the conversation. "And that would also explain the weapons stockpile at the drilling site. They were preparing to hold their ground if things didn't go their way."

"Exactly. The commander of your raid assumed that was the case as soon as those weapons were uncovered. That's how we got started down this path," Abril confirmed.

As the meeting drew to a close, the two sides agreed to share crucial information moving forward. Jenn and Castillo stepped out, their minds racing with the implications of the conversation.

Back in the car, Castillo reflected, "That was enlightening for both of us. I hope they appreciate what we did for them."

"Pfftt! I'm not holding my breath," Jenn responded, her skepticism palpable.

Watching the traffic as he drove, Castillo threw out a casual thought. "It's curious that Interior was going to cancel the Aspire contract, then Aspire tried to hire a bomb delivery to the minister's house, but the Aspire executive is the one who ended up dead. Is it possible the attacks were going both ways?"

"You think Interior could have done the same thing?" Jenn asked.

"I'm just considering all the options. But, for now, I'm taking you back to Hotel Quito. You heard the feds. The murder is still our investigation. You've got the best leads, and I'm sure someone in that group is involved."

"Thanks, Chief." Jenn felt a mix of pride and pressure. "I'll find them for you."

"Moving on from the federal details, here's some info from our talented medical examiner." Castillo couldn't help but chuckle as he said it.

"Because he's been so helpful so far," Jenn quipped sarcastically.

"This time, it's better. He says there are definitely two causes of death. The corpse had an injection site in the thigh, and the insulin levels were much higher than the C-peptide levels, which indicates the introduction of external insulin. The victim wasn't a diabetic, so someone else injected it."

"That points back to my veterinarian with the pharmacy in her suitcase," Jenn concluded, her theory gaining traction as she remembered the vial of insulin she had found in Karen's bag.

"Exactly what I thought."

"And what's the second cause?"

"The corpse has two tiny bruises on the neck, exactly over the carotid arteries. It's not like a full throat chokehold, but more like someone placed their thumbs gently on the arteries and waited for the blood flow to the brain to stop, leading to unconsciousness or death."

"Is there any DNA on those spots?"

"All he found was a trace sample of latex, like from a pair of latex gloves. So, the killer knew not to leave those clues for us."

Jenn pondered for a moment. "You can't choke someone to death with two gentle fingers unless they're already drugged. So, maybe the killer was just making sure, polishing up their work, ensuring the victim died even if the insulin alone didn't do the job."

"Possibly." Castillo nodded, intrigued by the hypothesis. "But then, why was the body in the shower?"

Jenn didn't have an immediate answer for that one. The placement of the body still perplexed her, hinting at another layer of the mystery to be unraveled.

CHAPTER 24

MARKET FINDS

Jenn stepped into the bustling lobby of the hotel where the air was thick with the sounds of travelers and the clink of glasses from the lobby bar. At a table near the center, she noticed a group of her runners, their faces animated and bright. They had laid out a veritable treasure trove of shopping finds across the top of the table, each item sparking discussions and laughter.

"Look at this sweater! One hundred percent alpaca wool and just twenty dollars," one exclaimed, holding up a soft, intricately patterned garment.

"Leather purse, thirty dollars," another chimed in, displaying the accessory's fine craftsmanship.

"For ten bucks, I got a dozen of these cute alpaca keychains," a third added, spreading them out like playing cards.

These prices were a dead giveaway to Jenn. They hadn't splurged at the hotel gift shop; they'd ventured to the La Mariscal Artisan Market. It was a vibrant hub for locals and tourists alike; the market sprawled across several city blocks, its stalls bursting with colorful clothing, handcrafted jewelry, and an array of eclectic souvenirs. The air there was always filled with the lively haggling of seasoned shoppers.

Among the merry group, Jenn's gaze settled on Karen, now her prime suspect. The urge to take Karen straight to the police station bubbled up inside her, but the implications of exposing her undercover status stayed her hand, not to mention the upcoming leg of the trip to the Galápagos Islands—a much-needed respite she was unwilling to jeopardize.

"They've struck gold," a familiar voice observed from over her shoulder.

Turning around, Jenn found Tatyana approaching, her arms laden with her own market spoils. "I see you have, too," Jenn replied, acknowledging the haul.

"That market is amazing. Literally thousands of things that are perfect for tourists. And so cheap," Tatyana remarked, and then, with a flourish, she placed a straw fedora on her head. "Ten dollars. And I'll need it for cover on the islands. I hear it's hotter there than in the jungle."

Jenn nodded in agreement. "This time of year, absolutely. But it's not summer yet, so it's still enjoyable most of the day."

"I can hardly wait to see the tortoises, iguanas, and penguins. Do they really swim where we can see them?"

Having vacationed on the same island before, Jenn confirmed, "You'll see them as soon as we get to the boat transfer area."

"Iguanas swimming in the ocean?" Tatyana sounded incredulous at the idea.

"Yep, all day, every day."

Tatyana, a tall redhead with a blue-eyed gaze that seemed to pierce through the bustle of the lobby, paused and looked reflective. "This is a big reason I came on this trip. You know, I worked in a zoo in Russia before moving to America. We had penguins, boobies, and iguanas, but all in small enclosures. It was kind of sad for them."

"I didn't know we exported our blue-footed boobies."

"You don't, not anymore, at least. But fifty years ago, they were available for the taking. So, the zoo keeps them alive and breeds them." Tatyana's voice held a touch of melancholy as she recounted these details, her deep love for nature evident in her tone. Shaking off the nostalgia, she turned her attention back to the lively table and moved to join the ongoing exchange of stories and laughter.

At that moment, Jenn spotted Joe and Christie, who had just entered the lobby. She decided to have a talk with them if they were willing. "Could we have a moment without your lawyers?" Jenn asked the couple.

"Maybe. What's it about?" Joe answered. Christie just glared and remained silent.

"I just wanted to tell you we've settled the details with the explosives. We know where they came from. We know who the delivery person was. So, you're not a suspect anymore." Since Jenn was developing a genuine attachment to the entire group, she added, "Sorry about tainting your vacation, but it's part of my job."

Joe relaxed visibly. "Well, that's a relief. I don't even want to know any details. We'll keep Toni and Lisa on retainer until we're out of the country, though, just in case."

"If you like. By the way, we're still working on that murder. So, if you remember anything, let me know."

With the day drawing to a close, Jenn prepared for the logistical challenge awaiting the group the next morning. The staff meeting outlined the intricate dance of transportation they would undertake to get thirty tourists from Quito to the remote Isla Isabela. The plan detailed a sequence of buses, planes, and boats—a testament to the complexity of travel in Ecuador.

As the meeting ended, Jenn couldn't help but find humor in the upcoming journey. "Welcome to your free vacation," she quipped, a smile playing on her lips as she anticipated the adventurous, albeit comically complicated, day ahead.

CHAPTER 25

MINGLING

J enn was the last to step onto the bus, the pale glow of the hotel's neon sign flickering in the predawn darkness. At three in the morning, the air was thick with sleepiness, the group's collective exhaustion palpable. No one craved conversation or snacks; they sought only the solace of sleep during the hour-long journey to the airport. Traveling from Quito to the Galápagos required a very early start.

Finding the last vacant seat, Jenn settled in beside Toni, the sharp-witted New York lawyer. She braced for an inquisition about Joe and Christie, but fortune was in her favor—the lawyer was already surrendering to sleep, her head tilted back against the headrest.

Jenn leaned back herself, her body relaxing as the bus hummed along. This week had been a whirlwind of activity, and today was a brief respite before the storm resumed.

A jolt of a dream—Castillo demanding answers—snapped Jenn awake. She blinked into the darkness; the bus was silent, save for the soft, rhythmic breathing of her companions. Only minutes had passed, but her detective instincts were already flickering back to life.

Her gaze drifted to the floor, landing on Toni's day bag nestled between their seats. A detective's curiosity never rested. Ensuring Toni was still lost in slumber, Jenn stealthily hooked the bag with her toe, drawing it closer. Under the guise of adjusting her seat, she slowly unzipped the bag, the sound almost imperceptible.

Jenn draped her jacket over her lap and the bag, her fingers delicately exploring the contents. She deciphered the shapes in the dark—clothes on top, likely a change for the day, and beneath that, the unmistakable edges of a book or notepad. But deeper still, her fingers brushed against something unexpected, yet familiar. The touch of crisp paper edges—stacks of them—told her all she needed to know.

Withdrawing her hand, she carefully nudged the bag back to its original spot. Jenn knew the feel of bundled cash all too well; those were undoubtedly bricks of hundred-dollar bills. By her estimate, Toni was transporting at least $80,000. What kind of vacation required that kind of spending money?

Pulling out her phone, Jenn messaged Castillo with her findings, her mind racing with the implications. She leaned back, her eyes wide open now. Rest was impossible with the wheels of her mind turning; a killer and a cash mule were aboard, and she was in the middle of them.

The bus trundled on; its occupants oblivious to the detective's silent machinations.

As dawn broke and the bus neared the airport, the interior lights flickered on. Patricio's voice crackled through the intercom, "Good morning, everyone. We'll be unloading shortly. Please ensure you have all your belongings."

Toni awoke, her gaze sharp and calculating as she fixed Jenn with a suspicious look. "What're you doing here? I know who you really are," she accused, and her voice was low but fierce.

Jenn returned the gaze with a calm smile. "Your clients are off the hook. They won't need you anymore."

"I'm still their lawyer. Don't talk to them unless I'm present," Toni snapped, clinging to her professional façade.

Jenn merely nodded, unconcerned by the American's legal argument.

Moving the entire group through an airport had become routine by this time. Everyone knew their role, waiting for their host and guides to provide tickets and instructions through the security maze. Once everyone was aboard the plane and bound for the Galápagos Islands, Jenn sought out Carlos, needing to vent to him to help piece more of the puzzle together.

Carlos greeted her with a grin, his laptop open to an array of photographs. "Look at these shots. Patricio thinks they're magazine-worthy," he boasted lightly, scrolling through images.

Jenn stopped him as the pictures flickered past. "Wait, how do you have these pictures from the opening reception? We weren't part of the group yet," she questioned sharply.

"Oh, Allen and I swapped folders. Now, we both have a complete set," Carlos explained, oblivious to Jenn's growing suspicion.

As they reviewed the photos, a few shots from the kickoff dinner captured Jenn's attention. In the background, the elegance of Aspire Oil executives contrasted starkly with the casual attire of the runners. Some runners, like Karen the vet and Tatyana, were mingling with the well-dressed figures.

Jenn leaned in, her eyes narrowing as she pieced together the unusual interactions. "So, the two groups *did* intermingle that night. Maybe just for a few minutes, but long enough," she muttered, her mind racing with the implications of this unexpected connection.

CHAPTER 26

AN EQUATORIAL WONDERLAND

Tatyana's excitement was palpable as she pointed frantically toward the crystalline waters. "Penguins on the right side!" she shouted; her voice laced with awe.

The group, momentarily forgetting their fatigue from countless transportation transfers since leaving Quito, surged to the starboard side of the taxi boat. The astonishing sight of penguins darting through the equatorial waters greeted them—an enchanting spectacle in the Galápagos Islands.

"Turtle," Carlos announced, leaning precariously over the boat's edge to capture the moment with his camera.

As the boat approached Isabella Island, the group was treated to a parade of biodiversity. The entry port was modest—a simple, wooden platform connected to the shore by a pair of weathered gangplanks. Yet the surrounding waters teemed with life. Sea lions frolicked nearby, while swimming iguanas and eagle rays glided beneath the surface, and a lone dolphin arched gracefully before disappearing into the blue depths.

Isla Isabella's natural bounty was a living tribute to the explorers who had chronicled its wonders over the centuries, from early Spanish adventurers to Charles Darwin, its most illustrious visitor.

Upon docking, Jenn remained vigilant, her detective's responsibilities mingling with her admiration for the surroundings. She kept close to Patricio, ready for instructions, yet her gaze frequently swept over the group. Karen had swiftly moved ashore, Toni lingered on the boat, and Jarrod unusually assisted with the luggage—a task typically reserved for staff.

Zuri rallied everyone on the dock. "It's a short walk up this road to our resort," she instructed. "We'll meet there for instructions and room assignments. Once you're settled, feel free to come back here to snorkel in the public cove."

Jarrod, intrigued by the prospect of snorkeling, quickly inquired, "Where?"

"Just across the water." Zuri pointed to a picturesque inlet just beyond the docking area. "You'll be swimming with all the creatures we saw on our way in. We've already arranged to have snorkel gear waiting for you in your rooms."

The promise of such close encounters with wildlife fueled the group's enthusiasm as they made their way to the resort, chatting excitedly about their plans.

Jenn's focus shifted as her phone rang—the first time she had signal since leaving the city. "Hello, Chief," she answered while stepping aside as the other group members walked by.

Castillo didn't waste a moment. "I checked out your lawyer. She entered the country on a work visa, then registered with the Banko Central del Ecuador as a certified courier."

Jenn frowned, unfamiliar with the term. "What's that?"

"It means she can transport and deliver sizeable sums of money legally. Her certificate covers up to one hundred thousand dollars. She's not smuggling; she picked up the cash at the Banco Pichincha in Quito. It's all in U.S. dollars."

"And she can just walk about with it in a backpack?"

"Yes, but she can't take it out of the country."

Frustration tinged Jenn's voice. "So, who's the money from? And who's she delivering it to?"

"The banks don't share that info, even with us. It's not illegal, but it's a strange coincidence, isn't it?"

After the call, Jenn trailed behind the group, her mind churning with the implications of Toni's role. Approaching Jack Hunter, she asked quietly, "Have you ever been hired as a certified courier for money?"

Jack's response was cautious. "Sure. It's one service I offer. Why do you ask?"

"And you're not working as a courier right now?"

"Well, it would be stupid of me to say yes to that question, wouldn't it?" His tone was evasive. He added, "But if I was, I wouldn't even have admitted that I knew what a courier was."

"Thanks. Just curious." Jenn nodded, storing away the information for later.

Post-check-in, Jenn decided to immerse herself in the natural beauty the group was so eager to explore. Donned in a swimsuit and sandals, she returned to the dock where Tatyana was already waiting with infectious enthusiasm. "This is the most exciting part of the trip. You can't see some of these animals anywhere else. You're so lucky to have such easy access to them."

Jenn agreed, "Even Ecuadorian citizens are thrilled by this place. I've only been here once before."

Tatyana's mood darkened. "Your country needs to protect this ecosystem better than they're protecting the Amazon. Big oil and big shipping will destroy all of this beauty if you let them."

As they reached the snorkeling platform, a shout drew their attention. "Iguanas!" A dozen large, black-scaled iguanas were basking on the platform, undisturbed by the humans weaving around them. One, annoyed, ambled toward the water's edge and slipped in, its body undulating with ease.

"Oh, my God!" Tatyana exclaimed, leaping into the water after the iguana, her mask fitted snugly to her face.

The rest of the afternoon was a symphony of splashes and laughter as the group swam alongside the unique assemblage of Galápagos wildlife. Penguins flitted through the water with brisk elegance, turtles cruised the seabed, and rays cast shadows on the ocean floor, all within arm's reach. It was a rare communion with nature, unfolding in the heart of one of the Earth's most revered sanctuaries.

CHAPTER 27

VOLCANO ISLAND

As dawn broke over the enchanted Galápagos Islands, the air was thick with the salty scent of the Pacific and the promising excitement of the day. The previous day's casual swim among playful sea lions and majestic rays was just a prologue to the adventures orchestrated by Global Runners.

Gathered at the trailhead for the Sierra Negra volcano, the group listened intently as Zuri outlined the day's plans. Her voice carried over the gentle rustle of the wind through the sparse vegetation. "Today, we focus on the volcanoes that crafted these unique islands," she began, her eyes bright with the thrill of sharing this natural wonder. "We start with a run along the outer edge of Sierra Negra. The trail begins at a lush mango farm nestled near the peak and descends to the base, offering a gentle decline but still exposing us to the elements."

The group, equipped with hydration packs and sun hats, nodded as Zuri emphasized the importance of hydration. "It's hot and humid, with long stretches under the direct sun. Everyone must carry at least two liters of water. Remember, there's a refill point at four miles, and we'll have snacks and more hydration stations waiting at the finish line."

With a last check to ensure everyone was adequately prepared, Zuri signaled the start. Jenn, tasked today with snack and drink duties, watched from the sidelines. Her gaze followed the runners as they disappeared down the trail. Knowing this trail was open to the equatorial sun, she thought they would wish for the gentle rains and tree cover of the Amazon, even with its accompanying mud bogs. But the heat and humidity were part of experiencing everything her country offered.

An hour later, as the sun reached its zenith, the runners began to emerge at the finish line, each one a testament to the grueling challenge of the equatorial climate. "Whew! That was definitely hotter than the jungle," panted Dave, now seeking refuge in the shade. "No rain and no tree cover from the sun at all."

As the cluster of finishers grew, the group bonded in their exhaustion, supporting each other with water and shared relief in the coolness of the gathered shade. Their camaraderie was a silver lining to the demanding conditions they had just endured.

Start to finish was one hour for some and two hours for others. When everyone was finished and rejuvenated by fresh watermelon, pineapple, and ample water, it was time to move on.

Zuri announced, "We're all gross and sweaty, but we've had time to recharge on snacks and water. Our transport trucks are waiting to take us directly to lunch at the Ceibo Nature Park. It's a combination of a garden, camping site, and café. We'll get some proper food in the shade and relax a little. Then we're off on our afternoon tour."

After lunch, the group embarked on a driving tour of the caldera of Sierra Negra, guided by a local ranger. As the rugged terrain unfolded before them, they learned of the volcano's temperamental nature. Just a decade ago, an eruption had forced the evacuation of a nearby town and endangered some of the iconic Galápagos tortoises. The ranger recounted the dramatic rescue operations, where helicopters had airlifted the massive, endangered animals to safety. They had saved two dozen of them, many with lava burns etched into their thick shells. Sadly, they had also counted many more that had died from their injuries. The population in the area was still recovering from the incident.

Jenn recalled the vivid news footage of these events that she had seen on television. Though it had been years, the images were still fresh in her mind. *The beauty of the Galápagos is inextricably linked to its volcanic origins, a source of both creation and destruction*, she mused.

Stella stood on the edge of the volcano, looking down into the enormous caldera. "It's not what I expected. In the movies, you stare down into a boiling pit of lava that's just about to shoot up in your face."

The ranger heard comments like this one often. "Señorita, we are very lucky that it does not look like that now. The heat would be too much to bear, and the fumes would be toxic. The volcano is still active, but like most in the world, that means it erupts once a decade, or once a century. Preferably the latter. As I described on our way up here, Negra last erupted in 2018. But that was minor compared to centuries past." He pointed to the opposite edge of the volcano's cone. It was over five miles away. "This cone is the largest in the world. Most of it has not seen lava in centuries, so it has had time for the vegetation to reclaim the surface. It looks like a valley between mountain ridges."

Waving his arm to encompass half of the horizon, Dave asked, "So, this whole enormous, concave piece was once the source of a lava eruption?"

"Sí, señor. That is what formed this part of Isla Isabela." Turning slightly, the ranger pointed to one barren spot in the caldera's floor. "You see the steam rising from that bare spot of earth? That steam is from molten lava far below the surface. It is potentially where the next eruption will emerge, but it could also come up anywhere. Volcanoes are very temperamental and difficult to predict, like my wife." Everyone had a chuckle at the joke.

Stella pointed to the barren area. "What are those buildings down there?"

"Those are the remains of a sulfur mine. Sulfur was a valuable export from the island until the 1950s. The mine was closed when it became too dangerous to operate and the price of sulfur declined. Today, we make more revenue from showing it to tourists than we did from selling the material."

The ranger turned around and pointed to the horizon behind them. "If you look in the other direction, you can see the peaks of two more volcanoes that contributed to the creation of Isabela. These spewed out enough lava in centuries past that they grew from several small islands and merged into the one big island that Isabela is today."

Everyone in the group was busily taking pictures of the volcanic mountains thrusting up to meet the clouds that drifted lazily across the island.

CHAPTER 28

CORNERED SUSPECT

As the sun dipped below the horizon, casting a golden glow over the landscape, Jenn's thoughts turned from the natural wonders of the day to the darker task at hand. Now that they were back at their resort, it was time to confront her prime suspect in the troubling investigation that had shadowed their journey.

"Carlos, you wait out here. I'm sure I won't need help, but just in case." Her partner stepped back into the shadows to wait.

She approached Karen's cabin just as the sky turned a deep indigo. The knock on the door was met with a swift response, the curtains whisking open as the door unlatched.

"Hello, Karen. May I come inside?" Jenn's tone was calm, but her eyes were sharp, observant.

Karen, visibly nervous, stepped back to allow the detective to enter. "I explained that all the drugs are just for the animals," she blurted out, and Jenn could tell that her voice was tinged with anxiety.

"But that's not entirely true, is it?" Jenn's question hung in the air as she walked over to Karen's day bag, left carelessly by the door.

"What do you mean? You saw the bottles."

"I saw the ones you wanted me to see. But we didn't do a thorough search, did we?" Flipping the bag, she reached for a zipper around the bottom, one that most of the runners never used. "What's in the bottom pocket of your bag?"

"What? Nothing. I didn't even know that was on the bag." Karen had become noticeably agitated.

Jenn pulled the zipper back just as she had during her bus search several days earlier. Reaching inside, her fingers found what she was looking for. She extracted the bottle and held it up with a questioning look at her suspect.

"Then what's this doing inside?" Looking at the bottle, Jenn continued. "It says 'insulin' here on the label. What would a vet need insulin for in Ecuador? Were you expecting to encounter diabetic dogs?"

"That's not mine! I don't know how it got in there." Karen's eyes were wide with fear.

Jenn didn't know what to expect from a cornered vet, but she had plenty of experience subduing large men and was sure she could handle anything this woman could dish out.

Holding the bottle up to the light, Jenn continued, "And I can see that more than half the fluid has been used already. Someone received a very large dose. Perhaps a lethal dose." She looked at the other woman, hoping she would break.

"No! I didn't! That's not part of my kit," Karen protested.

"You can explain that to the feds when they arrive. They'll be here soon to take you back to Quito. You'll find the island jail quite primitive until then."

Tears streamed down the woman's cheeks. "No! I just wanted to help a few animals. I didn't bring insulin with me. That bottle isn't even for animals. I can't get that in my practice. That one is just for humans."

"How can you tell the difference?" Jenn asked.

"It's too big. Dogs don't get that much product. Plus, it's not from my supplier. Just compare the labels. It's not mine," Karen pleaded.

Jenn decided she needed all the drugs as evidence, anyway, so she said, "Show me."

Karen was quick to produce the case of vials that Jenn had seen so many days ago. "See, all my supplies are labeled 'Animal Pharmetic.' And they say 'For Veterinary Use Only.'" Pointing at the insulin, Karen asked, "What does that bottle say?"

Jenn examined the label. "Southwest Pharmaceutical Industries. It's from Phoenix, Arizona." Jenn looked up.

"I'm from North Carolina, all the way across the country. I couldn't order from them if I wanted to." Then a realization passed across Karen's face. "That's the company Tatyana works for. That's hers, not mine. She must have planted it in my bag." For the first time since Jenn had walked in, Karen sounded like she had found a ray of hope. "Yes. That's hers. You go ask her who she works for. You'll see."

Jenn had heard plenty of criminals explain why the drugs they were carrying didn't belong to them. Karen's story didn't sound like that. It sounded true. It was helped by the fact that Jenn didn't need to ask who Tatyana worked for. She'd seen the woman's rain jacket with the Southwest Pharmacy logo emblazoned on it.

Jenn looked her suspect in the eye and said, "I might believe you. So, I'm going to give you a choice. You can either spend the night in jail, or you can give me your passport until I can sort this out."

Jenn left the room with Karen's passport in her pocket. Waving to Carlos, she said, "Come on, we need to find Tatyana."

CHAPTER 29

AMONG THE BLUE-FOOTED BOOBIES

Jenn and Carlos left the dark shadows of Karen's room and navigated the wooden walkway to Tatyana's quarters. She rapped on the glass door but received no reply. Peering through, Jenn could see a chaotic scatter of clothing and shoes, evidence of habitation, but the room itself was deserted.

Testing the island's unique brews, no doubt, Jenn mused, recalling the island's famed local brewery, where the crew often gathered. She considered waiting, but dismissed the idea. Tatyana could be hours. It would have to wait until tomorrow. With the ocean encircling them, there was no escape from the island.

The absence of Tatyana at breakfast spiked Jenn's worries. Had her quarry sensed danger and vanished? Jenn approached Zuri, her voice tinted with concern when she said, "Zuri, I haven't seen Tatyana since last night. Is everything all right with her?"

Zuri's laughter cut through the morning air, light and carefree. "Oh, she was more than fine last night. We were all at the brewery, and she was dancing the night away. She was still there when I left."

"And she's joining us for the trip today?"

"Absolutely," Zuri confirmed with a nod, and her eyes were bright. "She wouldn't miss it for the world."

Zuri then turned to address the group, her voice carrying over the gentle sea breeze. "Today, we're exploring the ancient lava tubes and the cliffs above them. It's a haven for the blue-footed boobies. So, gear up with sturdy shoes and swimsuits!"

As the staff members congregated, ready for the day's adventure, Jenn felt excitement and frustration. Tatyana was conspicuously absent from the group heading to the dock. Jenn wondered, *Has someone tipped her off?*

At the dock, Jenn enlisted Carlos's help, his camera always ready at his side. "Carlos, keep an eye out for

Tatyana. I need to confront her today, possibly even hand her over to the local authorities."

Carlos, ever observant, pointed his camera toward a snorkel boat and captured a snapshot. "You mean, like already on that boat over there?"

Jenn's gaze followed the direction of his lens. There she was—Tatyana boarding the vessel, stashing her bag, ready for the day. Jenn rushed to join, but the dive guide halted her. "Sorry, señorita, this boat is full. You'll be on the next one. Don't worry, everyone gets equal time in the water." His smile was reassuring, but Jenn was plotting her next move.

Across the water, Tatyana caught Jenn's stare and waved, a grin spreading across her face. "This is going to be incredible," she called out before turning back to her companions.

The journey to the snorkeling site involved three boats, weaving a path through the azure waters. They detoured around Blue Foot Rock, a sanctuary for nesting birds and sunbathing sea lions, much to the delight of everyone snapping photos.

Upon reaching the rugged lava shores, the guide briefed them. "We'll start on the rocks. Watch your step and keep your cameras ready for the boobies and the cacti. Later, we'll meet the sea turtles in the water."

The group dispersed, eager to explore. Jenn kept her eyes peeled for Tatyana, eventually spotting her across a precarious lava bridge. The rocks were jagged, threatening to trip the unwary with their sharp edges.

Catching up to her target, Jenn confronted the other woman. "I've been looking for you."

Tatyana gestured grandly at their surroundings. "And here I am, in this breathtaking place."

Jenn cut to the chase. "I found a bottle of pharmaceutical insulin from your company. What do you know about that?"

"No drugs on me. Where did you find that, Detective?" Tatyana's tone was cool, her gaze steady.

Jenn blinked, surprised. "You knew? How?"

"People talk over drinks. I listen." Tatyana's smirk was slight but telling. "Why is a Quito detective tailing us?"

"You know why. I'm looking for the person who administered a fatal insulin dose to Emilio Ortega. Perhaps a tall, red-headed Russian who caught his attention?"

Tatyana scoffed. "Why would I want to kill him? I'm just here for a vacation."

"But you knew about the oil drilling in the Amazon. You couldn't stop it, but you could take revenge on those destroying the environment you cherish," Jenn pressed.

"Creative, but wrong," Tatyana retorted, unflinching at the accusation being thrown her way.

"You could have gotten away with it if you had disposed of the bottle, instead of trying to frame it on a veterinarian," Jenn finished. Her voice hardened at the knowledge that she almost fell for the scheme and arrested the wrong woman.

"Yes, I suppose that was going too far. But when Karen said she had supplies for treating the poor animals here, the idea just sprang into my head." Tatyana's expression shifted subtly, from amusement to a slight unease. "It seems you have me figured out. Now what? You're going to arrest me on these craggy shores?"

Jenn was taken aback by the easy confession she just heard, but she didn't want to leave any room for doubt that Tatyana was guilty. "And then you followed up by choking him to make sure he was dead."

Tatyana looked shocked. "No. There, you are mistaken. Persuading Señor Ortega to take a quick trip up to his room was easy. Anyone could have done it. You could have done it. Once we were there, a swift jab in the thigh, and I was done. I waited long enough for the drug to make him disoriented so he couldn't call for help, then I left. I had to get back to the kickoff dinner."

"And you're confessing all this to me?"

"What can you do out here? Do you have a gun and handcuffs tucked into that little swimsuit of yours? I don't think so." Tatyana laughed at the powerlessness of the lone detective standing on lava rocks in the ocean. "Let's enjoy nature, honey. You don't have any power or authority out here." With that, the confessed murderer walked away to photograph blue-footed boobies.

After an hour of exploration, the guide called, "Everyone back on the boats. We're moving to our snorkeling location!"

As they boarded their separate boats, Tatyana waved at Jenn across the water separating them. This time, it was less friendly and more taunting.

The detective worried that her prey was far too confident. It was true, Jenn couldn't do much out here. But once back in town, she could easily detain the woman with the aid of the local police.

CHAPTER 30

LOST

The brisk, refreshing waters of the equatorial Pacific enveloped the group as they slipped over the side of the boat near Isabella Island. Once runners, they had now transformed into eager snorkelers, their bodies buoyant in the clear, blue expanse that stretched beneath them.

The underwater landscape here was a sanctuary for turtles, making sightings almost commonplace. Each snorkeler floated above the seabed, enchanted by the sight of these majestic creatures. Their slow, graceful motions painted a serene picture as they meandered across the rocky ocean floor, feasting on the abundant algae there.

Before this aquatic ballet began, their guide had laid down the law of the land—or rather, the sea. "The first rule is, don't touch the turtles. This ocean is a national sanctuary," he had declared firmly. "The second rule, stay together. The lava tubes along the shoreline are a maze. It's easy to get lost. Third, return to the boat in one hour." His last words, punctuated with a smile, were, "Now, get wet, and have fun!"

Under his vigilant eye, they explored the key habitats as he ushered them from one bustling turtle congregation to another. Some of the more adventurous snorkelers ventured into the shadowy realms of the lava tubes, their interiors sculpted by ancient flows of molten rock.

Stella engaged in a gentle underwater dance with a curious turtle, mimicking its movements in a synchronicity that felt almost choreographed. Meanwhile, Rogerio and Allen, equipped with waterproof cameras, delved into the dimly lit caverns, capturing the ethereal beauty of this submerged world.

Their explorations were filled with child-like wonder, each discovery met with bursts of silent excitement. It was Eva who broke the spell, her head surfacing as she called out, "Manta ray!" Her voice drew the group's gaze as she chased the elegant creature, her strokes strong and determined.

In a secluded niche, Allen encountered a different marvel—a complete turtle skeleton, its bones bleached white by time, lying in solemn repose. The scene was stark, poignant, and strangely beautiful, the remains undisturbed in their natural tomb. Respecting the gravity of the find, Allen filmed quietly, choosing not to disturb the peace of the animal's last resting place.

As the allotted hour drew to a close, a ripple of messages passed among the snorkelers. It was time to return to the boat. They emerged from the water, their faces alight with the thrill of their encounters.

"How did everyone enjoy that?" the guide asked as they clambered aboard, dripping wet and exhilarated.

"Beautiful," was the unanimous response, a simple, yet profound reflection of their shared experience.

However, the mood shifted abruptly as Oscar's voice cut through the chatter, laced with anxiety. "Where's Eva? Where's my wife?"

"I'm sure she's here," the guide reassured him in a calm voice. "Maybe she returned to the wrong boat. I'll radio them and check."

Tension hung in the air as the captains checked their passengers. The guide's next words carried a weight of concern. "Oscar, she's not on any of the boats. She must still be among the rocks. It's possible to get lost in the maze."

"I'm going back in," Oscar declared, already reaching for his fins.

"No, no, señor," the guide intervened. "We don't rescue that way. That will only lose another swimmer. We know these rocks very well. The boat can take us to where she is likely to be."

Skillfully, the captain navigated through the perilous rocky outcrops. Eventually, they spotted a private vessel with a solitary figure waving at them frantically. As they drew closer, Eva's voice carried across the water, "Over here! I'm over here!"

Relief flooded Oscar's voice as they pulled alongside the boat. "Eva, what are you doing over there? You scared me to death."

"You were scared? What about me?" Eva countered, her voice a mix of relief and frustration. "I was all alone in this maze. I climbed up on the rocks to look for you guys, but I saw nothing. Then, this boat appeared, and I swam for it."

Jenn, watching the reunion, felt a chill of unease, recalling Zuri's tale of a lost runner in Costa Rica. Even well-organized adventures could harbor risks.

Once they'd retrieved their lost swimmer, the boat captains counted their passengers again and exchanged the results. Everyone was accounted for. Then Jenn heard the radio message from another boat. "One of our passengers transferred to a private zodiac. She's been invited to the yacht parked further out."

Suddenly alarmed, Jenn asked, "Captain, who was it that transferred to the zodiac?"

He repeated the question on the radio and relayed the answer to her. "It was Tatyana. She said she'd meet us back in town later," the captain responded, trying to soothe her concern.

"What? No! Where?" Jenn couldn't hide her alarm as she watched the zodiac head toward the yacht. "What's the name of that boat?"

Raising binoculars, the captain answered, "It's the Serendipity II. Don't worry, she seemed to be friends with them. They'll bring her back."

Frustrated and anxious, Jenn dashed below deck to find her cellphone, but there was no signal at this remote side of the island. She sank down onto the deck, her head in her hands, overwhelmed by a feeling of helplessness as her quarry escaped her grasp.

CHAPTER 31

ATTACKED

Jenn returned to the resort, defeated. She had the murderer in her grasp, but she'd been so eager to confront Tatyana that she'd miscalculated the situation. In retrospect, she knew she should have waited until she had the woman cornered in her room, just as she had with Karen.

As the entire boat chatted excitedly about their experience swimming with turtles and Eva gave a blow-by-blow account of her ordeal through the lava tubes, Jenn could only worry about the horrible mistake she'd made.

Finding her roommate sulking, Zuri asked, "Jenn, cheer up. We had a fantastic day. What's the matter?"

Jenn's eyes betrayed a flicker of the turmoil within. She teetered on the brink of revealing her true identity, tired of the charade. Yet, her professional instincts prevailed. She cloaked her disappointment with a feigned worry. "Oh, sorry. I was just worried about Tatyana. She boated off with some strangers. What if they're dangerous? We don't know who they are."

Zuri's hand was comforting on her shoulder. "We don't, but she knew them. I heard her call out to someone named Mike as he approached. They looked like old friends."

"How did he know when and where to find her?"

Zuri shrugged. "I guess she told him the plan or called him when she finished snorkeling."

"There was no cell signal out there. I tried to call someone, too."

"It will be fine. You'll see. She'll be at dinner tonight," Zuri reassured her, then added with a whimsical sigh, "I just wish some rich yacht owner had invited me to lunch on his boat." After a quick pause, she then said, "Well, that sounds a little sketchy when I hear it myself."

As they approached the dock, Jenn excused herself with a murmur, heading straight for the resort bar. She needed some relief from the dread of reporting this news to Castillo.

Zuri was busy planning the afternoon run when Jenn headed back to their shared room. She slid back the door and stepped into the refreshing air conditioning.

There was a shuffle of feet and a flash of movement to her right. Her police training kicked in, and she ducked while simultaneously raising a blocking arm. It collided with the forearm of an attacker. Jenn spun under the person's forearm and punched toward where a body should be. Her fist connected with the soft abdomen of someone small.

There was an audible "oooff," as the punch forced the attacker to stagger back a step.

The distance allowed Jenn to straighten and face the stranger. "Alice! What're you doing?" Jenn was incredulous to find the small woman facing off against her.

Alice smirked and replied, "Just my job." She lunged again, and this time, Jenn could see that she held a long blow dart in her hand. Her mind flashed back to the darts that hit her door at the hacienda. This time, she had no question about whether the tip had been poisoned.

Jenn parried the blow and stepped sideways. She attempted to punch the woman again as her weight carried her forward. However, Alice was a trained fighter as well. Realizing that her dart was missing the target, she made a tight fist and delivered a snapping back hand punch to the side of Jenn's head.

Staggering, the two combatants faced each other again. Jenn's ears were ringing, but she realized she couldn't win this fight on the defensive, especially against a poison dart. Eventually, the tip would get her. She lunged forward and low, using her weight to push Alice backward as her hand shot up to gain control of the wrist with the dart.

Both women tumbled to the ground in a sprawl. Jenn retained her grip on the other's wrist. Both were spinning their legs, trying to ensnare the other, to gain an advantage by controlling their opponent's body. Jenn could tell that Alice was at least as well trained as she was.

After a few moments of wild thrashing and kicking, Jenn locked her legs around Alice's torso, giving her some control. But Jenn wound up on the bottom with the other woman poised above her, still trying to press the dart home.

Almost simultaneously, they both thought to punch with their free hand. Jenn thrust the heel of her hand high, connecting under Alice's jaw. Alice punched low, connecting with Jenn's midsection and driving the air from her lungs.

Jenn knew from the sound of clashing teeth that her blow had stunned the other woman. But Jenn's own loss of air at this exhausting stage of the fight was weakening her muscles' ability to resist.

At that critical moment, a fortress of muscle appeared behind Alice and grasped her hand in a steel grip. Jarrod lifted the woman from the pile on the ground, slapped her forcefully on the side of the head, and wrapped her in an embrace that stopped all movement.

Freed from her attacker, Jenn scrambled up and assessed the situation. Using both hands, she pried the dart from Alice's fist and tossed it into the corner.

"Thank God, Jarrod. She almost had me," Jenn said.

"I totally had you," Alice growled venomously, with defiance in her eyes.

"What the fuck is going on here?" Jarrod's voice carried both anger and confusion.

Jenn answered, "I actually don't know. But if you can hold her, I'll get the island police to come take care of her."

Alice answered, "Hunter, why're you siding with her? Maybe I'm the one who needs protection."

"Umm, because you had the dart, this is Jenn's room, and she's a cop," Jarrod answered matter-of-factly.

Alice spat at Jenn and then relaxed. She went silent, accepting her fate… for now. Under her breath, she muttered, "And you didn't have to hit me so hard."

When the local police arrived, Jenn identified herself as a Quito detective and explained that she was working with the federales on a murder case. Then she briefly summarized the attack. Jarrod confirmed her story.

The locals cuffed Alice and carried her to the small station in town with a single jail cell. Jenn promised to follow them as soon as she'd reported to her own superiors.

"What was that all about?" Jarrod asked.

"She said she was just doing her job. Does that make her a professional killer? I'm working on the murder of Emilio Ortega, the CEO of Aspire Oil. She must be tied to that." Jenn's mind was just beginning to work again. She remembered Tatyana had confessed to the insulin injection, but the Russian had denied choking Ortega. Could Alice be the choker?

Then she looked at Jarrod with surprise. "How did you just happen to arrive in time?"

"You two were making a racket, and we could hear it from outside. When I looked inside, it was clear this wasn't a lovers' quarrel." Jarrod glanced around the room and spotted the dart in the corner. "If she was trying to stab you with that, odds are it's poisoned." He collected the dart and handed it to her.

"I've got to report this and then go interview her," Jenn said. "You should go to the station and give a formal statement as well."

"Okay, I will. But can it wait until after the last run? We're going to weave through town and then finish with a mile along the beach."

"You still want to run after all that?" Jenn was incredulous.

"Sure. After all, this is my vacation. It's not a work detail for me," Jarrod defended.

"Fine, then, after the run. I need time alone with her, anyway."

"You won't be at the finish line to hand us juice and snacks?" Jarrod teased.

Jenn rolled her eyes. "Make my apologies to Patricio and Zuri. I think my snack service days are over, but don't tell them what happened. I'll handle that."

Jarrod nodded and left to prepare for the last run of the vacation.

CHAPTER 32

JUST BUSINESS

On the sun-drenched coastline of Isabela Island, the Global Runners convened outside their quaint seaside resort, marking the commencement of their last run. The route was a picturesque blend of culture and nature. It meandered through the small-town streets, veered onto a sandy access path, and culminated in a dramatic finish along the shoreline.

Absent from the group were Alice, confined behind bars, and Tatyana, who had escaped to the isolation of a luxurious yacht, distancing herself from the drama onshore.

As the runners poised at the start, the town seemed to embrace the occasion. Streets were cordoned off with "Do Not Cross" tape, which was fluttering like festive streamers in the sea breeze. A police cruiser idled at the front of the group, ready to escort the pack through the village. The energy was palpable. The community gathered to witness the spectacle of over thirty Americans dashing through their village.

As the runners received the traditional, "Global Runners… Go!" Jenn followed briskly down the street behind them. She was eager to learn more about what had motivated Alice's violent attack. She was planning her questions for the interview.

"Hello, Detective Moreno." The local captain of the station greeted her. "We have your assailant in our very best cell." He waved at the only cell in the building. Crimes on the island rarely called for strict incarceration.

"Thank you, Captain. May I speak with her?" Jenn asked, her tone professional, yet tinged with personal betrayal.

"Certainly," the captain replied before he and another officer discreetly exited to allow Jenn some privacy.

Inside the stark, whitewashed cell, Alice sat on a sparse cot, her demeanor calm, yet unreadable. "Alice, you surprised me," Jenn began, the weight of her words heavy in the air.

"That was the idea," Alice retorted. Her voice was steady, betraying no emotion.

"Emilio Ortega is dead. The coroner said he was gently and professionally choked. Just two thumbs on the carotid arteries to stop the blood flow to the brain. It's deadly within minutes." Jenn omitted the information about Tatyana and the insulin, hoping Alice would reveal details about her accomplice.

Alice nodded but said nothing.

"But a few mysteries need to be cleared up."

"Probably more than a few," Alice challenged.

"Probably. It appears that you're actually a professional killer for hire. I find that incredibly hard to believe."

"Why? Because I'm a woman? Because I'm small?" Alice challenged.

"Yes, those things are factors. But also, you've been so nice… well, until you tried to stab me."

Alice shrugged.

Jenn continued, "So, we figure you had no difficulty opening his hotel door. It's part of your professional skill set. Once inside, you found him in a strange situation." Jenn paused for a reaction.

Alice remained silent.

"Ortega was fully dressed in his formal tuxedo. But he was standing under the shower. He was disoriented and perhaps overheated." Jenn paused again.

"How did you know that?" Alice finally spoke, a flicker of surprise crossing her features.

This time, Jenn ignored the question. "So, instead of using your formidable skills to disable or seduce him, you found a much easier target. Maybe you actually supported and comforted him. But then, you laid one thumb on each artery. He didn't fight you at all. He simply melted into unconsciousness. All you had to do was hold the pressure for a few minutes, and the job was done. Then you waltzed out and returned to the party." Jenn stopped talking. She waited in silence.

"How did you figure all that out? No one else was in the room."

"Ecuadorian law enforcement is not as dumb as you apparently think we are. We have forensics just like the Americans." Jenn turned away, as if uninterested in the woman.

Alice responded, "Maybe you do."

Jenn returned her gaze back to the murderer. "How did you know he would be in the room?"

Alice laughed. "Easy. I saw Tatyana playing up to him. A blind person could guess how that was going to turn out. So, I followed them up to his room and waited in the hall. When they were finished with their little rendezvous, she left, but he stayed inside. As easy as that."

"But why? Clearly, you're a professional. Someone hired you to kill him. Who wanted him dead badly enough to go to all this trouble?"

"As you say, I'm a professional. Professionals don't divulge details like that. One doesn't live long if one forgets that rule."

"Who hired you isn't important to me. We have you, and that's as far as the Quito Policia's interest goes. If the federales want to know more, they're going to have to do that work themselves."

The mention of the federales visibly shook Alice, revealing a crack in her composed façade. Jenn observed this change with a mix of professional satisfaction and personal heartache.

Jenn could see the alarm on the woman's face. "Oh, yes, didn't I mention? The federales will be here in the morning to pick you up. We called them when the clues were falling into place." Jenn didn't mention that the plan was initially to take Karen into custody.

"Well, shit! That wasn't part of my plan."

"Your plan involved bribing the local police to let you go?"

Alice remained silent.

Changing to a more personal note, with pain in her voice, Jenn said, "Alice, you tried to kill me. I thought we were friends. We had such a good time on this trip.

I'm…" The detective was lost for words. Finally, she simply said, "hurt."

Alice answered, "I do like you, Jenn. Don't take it personally, it's just business."

Jenn felt the ice-cold frankness of that statement. It genuinely did hurt.

Exiting the building, she found Jarrod standing with the local cops at their truck. He was still dressed in his sweaty running clothes.

Seeing her, Jarrod said, "I've given them my statement. We were just discussing the race. It was quite an event. People turned out on their doorsteps and sidewalks to cheer us on. There was police tape across every intersection."

Jenn was still recovering from the shock of "it's just business." Trying to sound interested, she said, "I'm sorry I missed it. Did Patricio ask where I was?"

Looking at the police for support, Jarrod said, "We told him you had to take Alice to the infirmary. She had food poisoning." All three of them broke out laughing at this joke. Jenn didn't find it funny.

"Hey, you want to walk back? There's a finish line party on the beach."

"Sure, just a minute." Jenn turned to the police officers with a threat in her eyes. "The federales will be here in the morning to pick her up. She had better be in there when they arrive."

Looking at each other, both officers nodded, fully understanding the gravity of federal agents arriving on their little island.

Walking back to the beach resort, Jenn wondered about the rescue Jarrod had provided. "So, everyone could hear the commotion she and I were making during the fight?"

"Umhm," Jarrod confirmed.

"And yet, you're the only one who came running? There wasn't anyone else in the courtyard when the fight was over. Sounds suspicious to me." The detective looked at the security consultant, both recognizing the lie that had been uncovered.

"Well, maybe everyone didn't hear it. Maybe it was just me. Maybe because I was following you."

"And why would you do that?" She remembered the first time Jarrod had found her in his Amazon hut and had immediately mentioned his wife. She knew it wasn't a romantic interest.

Recognizing that he was caught, Jarrod said, "Captain Adriane Castillo. After our little exchange about the airport explosives, Castillo hired me to watch out for you."

"He hired you? With money? On a cop's salary?" Jenn sounded incredulous. She had some idea of how much a security consultant cost, and she knew a cop couldn't afford one.

"Not with money. If I agreed to protect you for the duration of this trip, he would make sure the federales didn't detain me for questioning. So, you're safe, and my vacation isn't ruined. It was a pretty easy gig until today. That dart could have gotten me, too."

Jenn gave Jarrod a sideways glance. She wasn't certain how she felt about this development. Castillo didn't think she could handle one runner-turned-murderer? It turned out he might have been right. Finally, she said, "Okay, then. Thank you. But I would have taken her down, eventually."

"Of course you would have." Then, Jarrod pointed toward the beach party, and that was the end of the conversation.

CHAPTER 33

FEDERAL DELIVERY

Jenn awoke to the golden light of the late morning streaming through the gauzy curtains of her room. Her body was a map of aches and bruises, each one a vivid reminder of her violent encounter with Alice the night before. Even though her physical wounds were apparent, it was the emotional exhaustion that weighed heavier on her. The adrenaline rush from the fight and the subsequent interview had drained her.

Patricio had shown an unexpected depth of understanding when she had asked to skip the day's excursion to Floriana Island. She had feigned a bout of the same food poisoning that had conveniently kept Alice confined to the infirmary. Their fabricated story was a necessary shield to protect the group from the unsettling truth that they had been in close quarters with a murderer.

Jenn wasn't sure how they were handling Tatyana's disappearance, but she decided that was Zuri's problem now.

With effort, Jenn peeled herself from the comforting embrace of her bed and dressed meticulously for her meeting with the federales. Today was not a day for casual island wear; the gravity of her appointment demanded more formal attire.

The rest of the travel group had already departed, and she had missed the communal breakfast. However, the prospect of coffee lingered in her mind as she checked her watch—she still had a spare hour.

Exiting her room, the late morning sun greeted her with its oppressive heat and building humidity.

"Morning, sleepyhead," Jarrod's voice floated from the hammock strung across the lush courtyard.

"What are you doing here? You're supposed to be on the morning excursion," Jenn asked, her brows knitting in confusion.

"Castillo hired me to watch over you, and I can't very well do that from another island, can I? If anything happened to you, he'd throw me to the feds," Jarrod explained, his tone only half-serious.

With a glance at his watch, he changed the subject. "So, what's the plan until the feds show up?"

"Coffee. Maybe breakfast. I'm still feeling the effects of yesterday's… workout," Jenn responded while touching a tender bruise.

"Are you planning to see Alice again?" Jarrod asked, and there was a hint of concern in his voice.

"No, thanks. I heard everything I needed to," Jenn said, her voice flat, the memory still fresh and painful.

The duo found a quaint cafe still serving breakfast. As they settled at a sidewalk table, Jenn's eyes inadvertently caught Toni browsing in a clothing store across the street.

"What's she doing here? Did she miss the boat, too?" Jenn murmured, more to herself than to Jarrod.

Jarrod followed her gaze. "I heard her tell Zuri she was feeling too tired for the trip. Mentioned something about seasickness, too."

"It's all a bit too convenient, isn't it? Her staying back with us… you, me, Alice," Jenn mused aloud, her suspicions creeping into her tone, but she left it at that.

Finishing her breakfast, Jenn announced, "Ten o'clock. Time to meet the feds at the dock." She motioned for him to follow her.

Jarrod held up a hand. "Not me. Remember, my job is to keep you safe. My payment is not meeting with the feds. I'm sure you'll be safe with them."

At the public boat dock, a sleek, black seaplane made a graceful landing on the water, drawing the attention of a gathering crowd. It took some time for the passengers to transfer to the local police boat and make their way to the dock.

"Detective Moreno, always in the thick of things, aren't you?" The commander who had led the raid on the Aspire Oil facility greeted Jenn as he disembarked.

"Small world, Commander. We've got the killer and her confession," Jenn replied, eager to update him.

Captain Castillo was next to step off the boat, and his presence was a surprise. "Hello, Moreno. Impressive work. How are you holding up after last night's fight?"

The unexpected knowledge of her fight with Alice caught Jenn off guard—clearly, Jack Hunter was doing his job by reporting the details to his client.

The commander wasted no time, and Jenn was thankful she didn't have to respond. "Let's go see our suspect," he said, leading the way to the waiting vehicles provided by the local police, who were eager to impress the federal team.

At the station, Jenn detailed the events leading to the capture. "Sir, I believe there were two people involved.

Tatyana administered the insulin, and Alice Lewis followed with the choking. Whether they collaborated or acted separately, I can't be sure."

The commander came to his own conclusion. "So, according to both confessions, Ortega was alive when Alice found him and dead when she left him?"

"Yes, sir."

"Then that makes her the killer. End of story. The other woman's involvement is incidental."

Jenn was surprised at his lack of interest in Tatyana. She glanced at Castillo for support, but he showed no sign of intervening.

The group then moved to the cells. "Señorita Lewis, you are now in federal custody," the commander announced to Alice.

"I'm ready. Let's go." Their prisoner sounded energetic, even happy about the process. Turning to Jenn, she said, "Sorry I roughed you up so badly last night, but it could have been worse for you." With a smile, she made a little jabbing motion with her hand, bringing back memories of the poisoned dart.

The entire group piled back into the trucks and headed to the docks once again.

As the federal officers pulled the handcuffed American from the truck, a small crowd gathered to watch the excitement. Word had spread that a federale airplane had arrived. Everyone wanted to see what they were doing here.

As the scene unfolded, whispers of "Americano" fluttered through the crowd, signaling that they were aware of who the woman was. Jenn watched as Alice was led away, her heart heavy with the grim satisfaction but tangled with unresolved threads about Tatyana's role.

As the team boarded the boat, the commander turned to Castillo and Jenn. "Moreno, you're staying here. Wrap up whatever undercover work you've been doing. Castillo, what about you? Are you staying or going?"

Without hesitation, he responded, "Staying."

"Fine. Enjoy a few vacation days." Then, forgetting the detectives, he turned his head and scanned the crowd on the dock. Spotting the person he was looking for, he pulled a keychain from his pocket and made his way into the crowd.

Jenn looked into the cluster of people herself. She saw where the commander was headed.

Arriving face-to-face with Toni, the New York lawyer, the commander handed her the keychain. She raised her phone and scanned the small token hanging from it, then examined the screen.

Confused, Jenn watched as Toni nodded in approval and then handed the commander her day bag. It was the same bag Jenn had searched on the bus ride to the airport.

Accepting the bag, the commander boarded the taxi boat, and it sped out to the awaiting seaplane.

Turning to Castillo, Jenn asked, "What just happened there?"

Raising his eyebrows, her chief just said, "Clearly, something you don't want to be part of."

Watching the boat as it sped away, Jenn thought she could see the large man handing the bag to a small woman, who was no longer wearing handcuffs.

Again, addressing Castillo, she said, "What the fuck is going on here?" Without waiting for an answer, she rushed to catch Toni as she walked back to town.

Within earshot, Jenn shouted, "Toni, hold up!"

The New Yorker turned, recognizing Jenn for the first time. "Hello, Detective Moreno. What are you doing down here? Just watching the excitement?"

Jenn said, "Listen, I know you're a registered courier with the central bank, and I know there was $80,000 in that bag you just delivered to the fedcrale."

"$100,000," Toni corrected, sounding arrogant as she did so.

"So, was that bribery money for the feds? Or what?"

"Detective, I'm only telling you this to forestall any idea you might have about arresting me. If you know I'm a courier, then you know that money is legally processed here in Ecuador. It wasn't smuggled in. I don't know what the money's for. I was told to carry it with me. At some point, my contact would present me with a green iguana keychain that had a tracking tag attached. I scan the tag. If it's the right number, then I turn over the bag. As simple as that."

"And you weren't suspicious that the exchange was on the public dock of a remote island? Or that the recipient was the commander of a federal task force?"

Toni chuckled. "I've done much stranger deliveries than that. And they didn't include a tropical vacation." Toni waved around at their surroundings.

Jenn was speechless. Following the trail of a killer as they traveled across the country had been challenging enough. Watching both of her suspects disappear via boat, and witnessing a money drop, was more than she could process right now.

There was a tap on her shoulder. Castillo said, "Let's get lunch and talk."

CHAPTER 34

COMPLETING THE PUZZLE

Jenn and Castillo found a small café for lunch, drawn by reports of its delicious food and reasonable prices. As they awaited their meals, the sizzling sounds and enticing aromas of grilling fish permeated the air. They watched the chef expertly maneuver red snapper on the huge grill at the front of the dining area, sparks occasionally flying up like tiny fireworks.

"Chief, this investigation has been exhausting. I don't know if I succeeded or failed with this case," Jenn confessed, rubbing her temples as weariness clouded her expression.

"Officially, it's a success. We have a confessed murderer in custody. We turned her over to the judicial system. Now, our work is done," Castillo responded, his voice steady, but his eyes betrayed a hint of doubt.

"Is it? My head is still full of the jumbled pieces." Jenn's voice cracked slightly, frustration clear in her knitted brows and in the way she fidgeted with the napkin in her lap.

Castillo watched her with concern. "Alice Lewis confessed to choking Ortega. Why would she do that instead of just denying her involvement?"

"I don't know. It was like she was bragging about it. After that, it was a slam dunk to turn her over to the feds. We didn't have to convince them to get involved." Jenn shook her head, remembering other cases back home where the local police desperately needed federal assistance but received none.

"They actually couldn't get here fast enough when you said you had the murderer," Castillo mused and leaned back in his chair, then stroked his chin thoughtfully.

"And there was a bag of money waiting for them when they arrived," Jenn added, her tone laced with sarcasm as she recalled the scene.

"About that money. I was able to talk to a friend at Banco Pichincha. He told me the money came from a law firm's account in Quito. Specifically, a firm that does a lot of work for the government."

"Which branch of the government?" Jenn leaned forward; her interest piqued.

"One guess who their primary client is," Castillo offered, and a wry smile played at the corners of his mouth.

The realization dawned on Jenn. "The Ministry of the Interior?"

"Exactly. Does that break open the piñata for you?" Castillo's eyes twinkled with the intrigue of the unfolding mystery.

Just then, a petite young woman arrived with their plates of food. The fish, fresh from the ocean, was accompanied by an array of vegetables from the local farms. The server placed the dishes before them with a polite smile and retreated.

Jenn's mind raced as she pieced together the complex puzzle. "Okay, so this is a long chain of events, but stay with me. Going back to the beginning, the Ministry of the Interior gave a contract to Aspire Oil to explore in the Amazon. Then, since this is Ecuadorian politics, let's assume that a bribe was involved to get that contract."

"That's a safe assumption," Castillo agreed and nodded slowly as he followed her logic.

"Now, what if the bribe wasn't paid? Or maybe another company offered a bigger bribe? Either works. The ministry decided to cancel the contract with Aspire.

Or rather, the minister himself made that decision." Jenn paused, her gaze distant as she visualized the scenario.

"Aspire got word of the impending cancellation. So, they took some of their explosives already in the country and hired an outside contractor to deliver a bomb as a message to the minister's house. Maybe they wanted to intimidate him. Maybe they wanted to kill him," Jenn continued. Her voice dropped to a whisper as the gravity of the situation settled in.

Castillo nodded along, absorbed in the narrative. "I'm following you. Someone at Interior gets wind of this and they realized they clearly had a problem on their hands. So, they struck back. They hired a professional killer to take out Ortega to show they can't be intimidated."

Jenn picked up the thread, a spark of appreciation in her eyes for Castillo's insight. "So, almost at the same time that Jack Hunter is supposed to be delivering a bomb, Alice Lewis is stalking Ortega. But Jack claims he doesn't do illegal jobs. Which we may or may not believe." She paused, then added with a lighter tone, "Oh, by the way, thanks for hiring Hunter to watch out for me. Alice might have succeeded in killing me with that dart if he hadn't stepped in."

Castillo smiled and his eyes softened. "It was the least I could do since I sent you out here alone." He'd felt guilty for not providing more support once he realized how dangerous this case was.

"So, back to our theory. Jack didn't deliver the bomb, but Alice succeeds at her hit on Ortega. Later, the feds discovered the bomb at the airport. They know it was from Aspire, and they knew about the pending cancellation of the contract. But with Ortega dead, they turn to his second in command and organized a raid on the executive's hacienda. When that turned up nothing, they targeted the drilling compound in the Amazon. That struck pay dirt. Not only did they find the matching explosives, but they uncovered a stash of weapons. Those suggested preparation for a big fight with the government if the contract was canceled." Jenn concluded with a satisfied nod.

Knowing the running group best, Jenn adds the last bit of details. "Alice Lewis signed up for this trip at the last minute. Her plan was to kill Ortega and then skip away across the country. She came and went under the cover of a large vacation group. Everyone was looking around Quito for clues, and she's been off in the mountains, then the jungle, and finally here on the islands."

Jenn chewed thoughtfully on her food, the flavors mingling perfectly on her palate, yet her mind was far from the simple culinary delight. "But that still leaves us with a loose end. Why did Alice try to kill me? I was still focused on Tatyana as the killer, which she was, indirectly."

The conversation paused as they ate, each lost in their thoughts, piecing together the tangled web of corruption, betrayal, and intrigue that had led them to this point. The gentle sea breeze and the occasional calls of seagulls overhead provided a stark contrast to the dark currents they were navigating.

Finally, Castillo asked, "How does your tall Russian fit into this mess? Who put her here?"

Returning from deep thought, Jenn answered, "Good question. She was a very outspoken environmentalist during the entire trip. And she didn't deny it when I accused her of taking revenge against Aspire for their destruction of the Amazon ecosystem. I think she's an independent actor in all this. Working from her own motives."

Castillo shook his head. "I don't buy that. Sure, it's something an environmental extremist might do. But then, there's her escape at the last minute. Who has access to a luxury yacht that can whisk her away right under your nose?"

Jenn replied hesitantly, "Another rich environmentalist?"

Again, Castillo shook his head. "You don't get rich enough to afford a yacht by saving the environment. What if that yacht belonged to one of the rival oil companies? Tatyana's fanatic enough to give Ortega a fatal dose of insulin, sure, but she had no way of escaping. So, she made a deal with another oil company to get her out. Possible?"

Jenn conceded his point with a nod. "That's possible, but still pure speculation. We don't know if another company is hanging around."

Castillo confirmed, "No, we don't. But if that exploration contract was in play, you can be sure those companies were nearby."

"This whole thing is mentally exhausting. So many players. So many possibilities." Jenn sipped her coffee as she stared at the peaceful street of the little village. They were blissfully ignorant of the drama that had come to their shores.

Castillo continued, "We're not done yet. You have a money courier here on the island. She was waiting for her contact to show up, but she had no idea who it would be. Big surprise, it was the commander of the federale team that has been involved in this case all along."

"Yeah, I didn't understand that at all. Why would the government use a law firm to arrange a money drop to a federal officer and do it all the way across the country?" Jenn did have a hunch about that, but she really couldn't believe what she might have seen.

Castillo, on the other hand, had been involved with the government for decades and had a darker opinion of what was possible. "I'll give you a theory. The minister of the interior hired their assassin, Alice Lewis. The minister put the payment in the hands of a courier, but he needed the case to be closed and for Lewis to disappear from the country. So, the federales and our friendly commander are her ticket off the island and the key to her payment. Your New York lawyer hands the bag of money to the commander, and when they're out of sight, he hands it to Alice Lewis to pay for her services and her silence."

Jenn asked, "So, she's not really under arrest? Then what happens to her?"

"Lost in the system. No one asks questions," Castillo concludes. "She'll be lucky to arrive in Quito alive. Maybe she gets shot trying to escape. Maybe she falls out of the airplane before they get to the mainland."

Jenn interrupted by saying, "Or maybe she knows her job better than that and has made arrangements for a disclosure if she goes missing. We'll never know which one."

"Exhausting," Castillo agreed.

Both of the police officers' gazes drifted down the quiet street. The meal concluded with both feeling a deeper sense of understanding. They left the café not just with satisfied appetites, but with one remaining step for wrapping this case up.

STAGED

In the commandeered dining room of the resort, Jenn convened a select gathering under the guise of a casual meeting. She began the conversation with a touch of formality. "Zuri, Patricio, allow me to introduce Captain Adriane Castillo of the Quito Policia Force. He joined us with the federal agents earlier today."

Zuri, her curiosity piqued, interjected, "I caught wind of all that when we got back from Floriana Island. What happened while we were gone?"

Castillo, with a reassuring nod, responded, "We'll clarify shortly. Please, let Jenn continue."

Regaining the group's attention, Jenn revealed her true identity. "I'm Jenn Moreno, not from the water department, but a detective with the Quito Policia Force. My apologies for the deception, but it was necessary for our investigation. You may have heard there was a murder at the Hotel Quito on the day of your arrival."

Patricio, connecting the dots, remarked, "I remember seeing that on the news. It involved someone from an oil company, right?"

With the scene set, Jenn dove into the intricate details of her investigation, capturing Zuri and Patricio's undivided attention. While preserving the confidentiality of sensitive information, she cautiously described the alleged actions of Tatyana and Alice.

Concluding her overview, Jenn invited questions. "I know it's a lot to take in. Do you have any questions?"

After a tense silence, Zuri was the first to articulate her shock. "So, you're saying we've been in the company of two murderers?"

"Alleged murderers," Jenn corrected. "But yes, that seems to be the situation."

"And their current whereabouts?" Zuri pressed.

Jenn recapped, "Alice is now in federal custody, headed back to Quito. Tatyana, however, escaped aboard a luxury yacht and hasn't been seen since."

The meeting spiraled into an intense, hour-long discussion as the expedition leaders grappled with the revelations.

Eventually, as the tension ebbed, Zuri sought confirmation. "There's no need to alarm our clients about this development, right?"

Castillo nodded. "Correct. The less they know, the better for everyone involved." He did not elaborate on how many clients already knew parts of this story.

"Good. Then, we proceed as planned to Quito tomorrow?" Zuri confirmed.

"Absolutely," Castillo affirmed. "Your journey will continue uninterrupted."

Relieved, Zuri proposed, "A drink, then? It's on Global Runners tonight."

As the tension dissolved into the night with casual drinks, Patricio floated an idea past them. "Jenn, Global Runners is returning in the fall. How about joining us again? For both the snack service and added security?"

Jenn chuckled, her eyes glinting with amusement. "You'd have to negotiate with my actual boss for that." She tipped her head at Castillo while her mind raced over the last two weeks. Hopefully, the fall trip wouldn't include rolling boulders, blow darts, venomous spiders, or wrestling with an assassin.

"And Carlos must come back, too. His photography is stellar," Patricio added.

Zuri, with a conspiratorial wink, agreed, "Absolutely, he captures much more than what most people can see."

The following morning, as dawn flirted with the horizon, the Global Runners assembled for their departure. Even Castillo was there, a last-minute addition to their return itinerary.

On the shadowy walk to the dock, Jarrod fell in step beside Jenn, his voice low. "How did it all pan out?"

Jenn, her tone mixed with intrigue and disbelief, shared, "Mostly as expected, but with a peculiar twist. After you broke up the fight with Alice, she called you Hunter. She knew exactly who you were. Why is that?"

Jarrod, his silhouette merging with the dim light, replied nonchalantly, "Probably did her homework. And about that fight—she paid me to intervene. She said I'd need to break up a fight in your room that evening."

Stopping dead in her tracks, Jenn processed the revelation. "So, it was all staged? She wasn't after me?"

"Staged, yes. Dangerous, potentially. But I wasn't about to take any risks. I don't think she expected to get head-slapped that hard," Jarrod admitted, grinning to himself.

Astonished, Jenn exclaimed, "She orchestrated her own arrest to get into federal hands?"

"Seems so," Jarrod confirmed.

Jenn, half-amused, yet exasperated, concluded, "And you helped her?"

Jarrod smiled slyly and shrugged. "It was just business."

As they approached the boat, the first rays of the sun pierced the horizon, casting a new light on their journey back, filled with as many questions as answers.

EPILOGUE

Jenn Morales resumed her role at the Quito Police Force after this wide-ranging investigation. However, her connection to the Global Runners remains unbroken. Each spring and fall, Jenn returns to the group, serving not only as their beloved "snack girl" but also as their security detail.

Carlos embraced a new chapter as a globe-trotting photographer for Global Runners. While he left his position at the Quito Police department, he continues to visit and occasionally assisted the department when he's in Ecuador. Together with Allen, their vibrant images capture the spirit of adventure and camaraderie at Global Runners' events worldwide.

Jarrod Turner, also known as Jack Hunter, found himself increasingly in demand as a security specialist, thanks to referrals from a mysterious supporter whom he suspects to be Alice Lewis, the elusive assassin. Despite the shadowy nature of his engagements, Jarrod's expertise in security continues to be his greatest asset.

Alice Lewis vanished under mysterious circumstances from custody in Ecuador. Although her body was never found, insiders confidently believe that Alice is alive, well, and has resumed her covert activities. Her disappearance remains a mystery.

Tatyana also faded into obscurity. However, eagle-eyed observers have spotted a tall, red-haired woman at various environmental protests around the globe, sparking rumors that the enigmatic Russian is still promoting her cause, albeit from the shadows.

Karen vonScheck… something has notably changed her travel habits. She no longer brings veterinary drugs on her vacation trips. Instead, she carries a kit of basic animal first aid supplies, ensuring she's prepared for minor emergencies without attracting the attention of law enforcement.

Sheryl Bear, tragically, was kidnapped at the conclusion of the trip. The location of the treasured stuffed animal remains a mystery, prompting Global Runners to offer a substantial reward for its safe return, no questions asked.

Global Runners Travel continues to thrive, adding new and exciting destinations to its roster each year. Since the thrilling events on their inaugural trip to Ecuador, there have been no more incidents of murder. But other adventures continue to unfold during these vacations.

BONUS:
JACK HUNTER,
ONE MORE MISSION

Join our newsletter community to receive an exclusive bonus, Jack Hunter's last surprise mission, before leaving Ecuador.

https://www.rddsmith.com/jackhunter

Also check out the Medical Thrillers by R.D.D. Smith

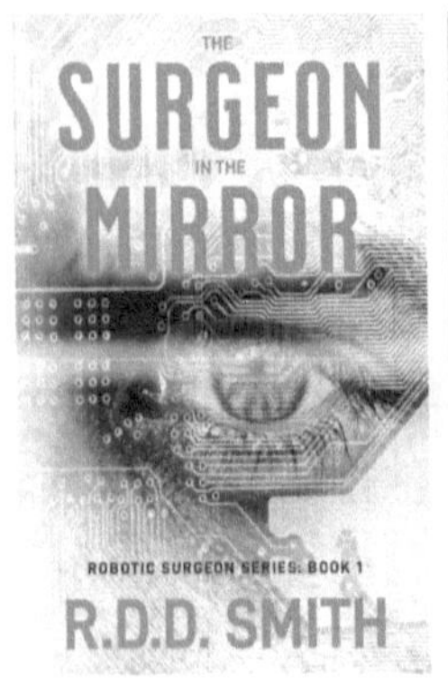

https://www.rddsmith.com/books

or

https://www.amazon.com/dp/B0C59ZRZDR

AI DISCLOSURE

The text of this novel was written by the human author. I used GPT-4 as a research tool to collect background information on Ecuador, its traditions, and cultures.

ABOUT R.D.D. SMITH

Dr. Roger Smith writes science-fiction, medical thriller novels featuring advanced surgical devices, AI, telesurgery, simulation, and speculative diseases. *Blood on the Equator* is his first murder mystery. It was inspired by his vacation trip through Ecuador, visiting all the sites included in the story. He was also part of a running tourist group, exactly as described in the story.

Prior to writing fiction, he enjoyed a goldilocks career in healthcare, government, and national defense. For ten years, he was a leading robotic surgery researcher, publishing his results in medical journals and speaking at surgical conferences. He spent four years in civilian government service, leading the technology innovation for all U.S. Army simulation systems. Prior to that, he was a vice president for multiple defense software companies.

Dr. Smith has received multiple awards for his innovations in robotic surgery education, training simulation, and software system development. He is on the faculty of the University of Central Florida's College of Medicine and the Institute for Simulation and Training.

He holds a Doctorate and MBA from the University of Maryland, a Master's from Texas Tech University, and a Bachelor's from Colorado State University.

He lives with his wife, dogs, and cats in sunny Florida, frequently escaping to cooler climes during the beastly Florida summers.

STAY IN TOUCH

Review:
Please leave a review of this book on Amazon or
your favorite book site.

Join Us:
Join our community of readers to receive fascinating
news related to the story.

www.rddsmith.com/free

ACKNOWLEDGMENTS

As an author, I am infinitely grateful to my readers who invest their time, money, and imaginations in following my stories and characters through their challenges, failures, and transformations.

First, to my wife, who has endured decades of fanatic immersion into whatever my latest passion is, most recently, these novels. Your patience, dedication, and love are appreciated every day.

For this first murder mystery, I am indebted to Vacation Races Global Adventures, for organizing the fantastic vacation that inspired the events in this novel. Special thanks to Cheri Santiego, Zoe Calcott, and Salem Stanley for creating a business, an adventure, a community, and a family all in one. Thank you to the inaugural group of runners in Ecuador for your enthusiastic encouragement as we created and discovered each chapter of this book together.

For my editor Kaitlin Travis, book layout artist Adina Cucicov, and the many advisors who made this book far better than I could have accomplished alone.

www.ingramcontent.com/pod-product-compliance
Lightning Source LLC
Chambersburg PA
CBHW061533210726
48287CB00006B/1941